Teenage Jesus

by Caleb King

"And the Lord answered me, and said,
Write the vision,
and make it plain upon tables,
that he may run that readeth it."

Habakkuk 2:2

Part One

1:1

So it's Saturday night in Nazareth, and our usual
gang is hanging out, looking for something, anything
to do. There's Eli, who's tall and skinny and fancies
himself a ladies' man, for no good reason. Oren, built
like a bear, but wicked shy with the girls. Tobiah and
Saul are the twins; both good guys, but a clear
division of Tobiah having the smarts and Saul having
the looks. Funny how that happens.

There's me, of course. I'm Joel.

And then there's Jesus. He doesn't always come with
us, but when he does, something unusual happens.
Like the time we got Oren's donkeys drunk so they'd
mate.

Oren's family had been waiting for years for their
"herd," as Oren called it, to increase with the
addition of a third donkey, but nothing was working.
We figured if, like one of us, the donkeys were
drunk, they'd be less picky. The problem was getting
that much wine. Since it's used every Friday night
and on special occasions, someone would notice if a
barrel of it was gone. None of us had much money,
except for Eli, but he's a cheap bastard and was
saving up for a new robe to wow the ladies. Like *that*
would be enough to make his skinny ass more
attractive.

So we're hanging out, like I said, and Jesus gets that funny look on his face. Like he knows something no one else does. Kinda weird. He says we need to go find a big bag to put the wine in. "What wine?" we all ask. He starts walking towards Tobiah and Saul's house, since their dad makes leather bags, the best in town. And we all follow, cause none of us has a better idea.

We snoop around the shop till we find this huge bag. Just about then, the twins' mom comes out swinging a frying pan, ready to belt whoever is robbing the shop. When she sees it's just us, she relaxes and offers to make us a snack. So, of course, we let her. She makes us this awesome meal, but then I almost puke from hearing way too many details about her giving birth to the twins. Gross. We head over to Oren's stable and quickly realize we should have hit up the twins' mom for the wine, even though she probably would have said no. Jesus stands up and says, "here, give me the bag." Of course, we all want to know what's up. He walks over to the well and starts filling it up with water. Tobiah lays into him about the uselessness of a bag of water for our mission, but Jesus just chuckles to himself, then looks over his shoulder and gives us one of his weird little smiles.

Filled up full, he tosses the bag to Saul, which knocks him on his ass, since he didn't see it coming. We all got a good laugh out of that. So Saul decides to take a swig, and he coughs and sputters and sits there looking shocked, which of course gets us all laughing again. Like I said, not the sharpest knife in the drawer. "It's wine!" he shouts. We all started making fun of him, but he gets all big-eyed and says, "I'm serious - taste it!" So Tobiah tries it and verifies. "It's wine alright. And good wine at that!"

None of us could make any sense of it, so we all tasted it. It was wine, alright. So we all tried a little more. At that point, the whole discussion about what the hell had happened just sort of disappeared. Who cares how it happened? It was wine! So we drank to our success. And then to the donkeys. "To the donkeys!"

I looked over at Jesus, but he kept looking at one of the other guys, avoiding my gaze. Did he have anything to do with it? I wondered if maybe the well had just suddenly started pouring out wine, but that didn't make any sense either.

At that point, it seemed kind of a waste to give the wine to the donkeys. They smelled *so bad*: no wonder they didn't want to mate. But it was getting late, and we needed to get them to seal the deal. So we all had one more swig and then
poured the wine onto the donkeys' tongues,

and they lapped it right up. Saul wanted another swig, even after the mouthpiece had been in a donkey's mouth, so we gave him crap about that. Such a tool.

The wine now consumed, not much happened with the donkeys. Eli said maybe some music would help put them in the mood. We were all feeling pretty darn good at that point, so Jesus busts out with a wedding song and we all joined in. Man, we must have sounded like asses ourselves. That's about when the neighbors started yelling at us.

So we giggled like girls and shooshed each other and lined up the male behind the female, and Saul started rubbing it's backend and saying all this stuff like, "Oh yeah, you like what you see, don't you; yeah, she's right there waiting for you; go for it, man, it's your family duty." We were *rolling* on the floor, which turned out not to be such a good idea as we were in the stable and there was dung all over and we wound up smelling as bad as the donkeys. But it was damn funny. Saul can be a tool, but sometimes he just busts us up.

So the male starts mounting the female and we start cheering him on, and I guess he was a little drunk, too, cause he's having a hard time standing on just his back two legs, and I thought I was going to burst it was so funny.

But he got the job done. The female was heehawing so loud, we didn't hear the neighbors anymore. It was kind of sick to stand there and watch, but hey - Saturday night in Nazareth, there isn't a hell of a lot else to do.

We all shook hands, feeling very proud of ourselves, having accomplished our worthy goal. We told Oren we hoped the baby didn't come out looking like him, and he started wrestling with us, and that was when we realized we smelled like the stable, so we decided to go down to the stream and wash ourselves off. Jesus said he was going to go home. I told him he smelled just like the rest of us, but when I went over to him, he didn't smell at all. So we said goodnight and went down to the stream.

We stomped our feet along the path to scare off snakes and walked right into the water. I guess it kind of sobered us up, too, cause we started wondering where the wine had come from. None of us could remember. Somehow I thought it had something to do with Jesus, so I made a mental note to ask him about it the next day.

Walking back home we were pretty tired and quiet, but still felt good. Every once in a while one of us would start snickering, then we all would. It didn't really matter what part of the evening anyone was laughing about, we all could think of something to get us going again without even talking about it. That lasted the better part of a week.

When the donkey was finally born, Oren named it after Saul, in honor of his hysterical coaxing that finally got the job done. Saul got all embarrassed about it, but I could tell he was psyched about being remembered for doing something funny rather than something dumb.

I never did ask Jesus about the wine. There were so many other weird things that happened with him, I just kind of got used to it.

1:2

I don't know what it is, but whenever our gang gets together, which is almost every night, we spend a good hour or two, if not the whole night, talking about what we should do. My dad says he and his friends used to do the exact same thing. My sincere hope is that in coming generations, we as a civilization will have progressed to the point where we don't waste so much time with crap like that. Drives me crazy.

So here's the usual drill. Eli always wants to go bother some girl that he says is "likin' me," which usually means she's just laughing at him. And that's usually Rachel, who he's had this crush on since they were born, practically. Of course, she can't stand him. He tries to act all smooth with the girls, but they know it's just an act, and not a very good one, either.

Tobiah, the smart twin, just wants to have discussions, typically about God and stuff. Shoot me now. Although he sometimes gets Oren going, it usually ends with Oren's argument falling apart, at which point Oren tackles and wrestles him. Saul, the twin with the looks, just follows along.

Jesus is only with us about half the time. When he's not with us, he's usually walking around on his own. Nice enough guy, but just this side of odd. I guess he's one of those sensitive types who likes to think about the world and how it works. Not me. I like to be around people, and I like to have something to do. My dad likes to tell the story that when I was a kid, he used to tie knots in rope for me to untangle, just to keep me busy. I still like to do that, actually. It's better than doing nothing.

So I don't really care what we do as long as it's *something*. Talking about it can be fun sometimes, but when it's just an endless string of "I don't knows," I can get pretty grouchy.

Like a couple of weeks ago, we were standing around one night, and having that kind of brain-numbing discussion, and I was about to lose it, and all of a sudden Jesus just tackles me. He pins me down on my back and just looks at me, with one of his weird looks. At first, I got kinda scared cause I thought maybe he liked me, the same way Ezra the basket-weaver's son
likes Saul? But then he said, "what good thing do you not have right now?" The way he said it really hit me. It's like all of a sudden I saw this overview of my life and how someday we'd all be married or move away, and we wouldn't be hanging out anymore. Then he got up and yelled "dogpile on Joel!" so I figured he was okay. *I* wasn't though, cause Oren landed on me first, and he is one big guy.

I'd have to say that of the six of us, Oren is probably my best friend. Eli is usually pretty cool and I've known him the longest, but he's all about the ladies.

I think he'd sell any of us out in a heartbeat if it meant one night alone with Rachel. Tobiah is a good friend, too, although he gets a little too intellectual sometimes and acts likes he's the expert on everything. Saul is like our collective little brother. Even though Tobiah beat him out of the womb by a just few seconds, we all think of him that way. Good guy, just a bit slow. All the girls think he's cute, but he's sort of oblivious to it.

Jesus is friends with all of us, but none of us more than the others. It's like he's the mortar for us bricks. Or something like that. All told, we make a pretty good wall.

This one time, Eli was so full of himself that he told us he could get a prostitute to give it to him for free. So of course, we called him on it. We'd all just put money down on the bet, and Jesus came walking up. When we told him what was going on, he just got this quizzical look on his face. But he came along with us.

It was well after sunset, and we headed for that part of town. At the end of the street where prostitutes hang out, Eli turns around and tells us all to stop following him or we'll look like a bunch of shepherds just back from the hills.

Tobiah: And how will we know that you really did get doinked for free, if we can't see what's going on?

Eli: What is the deal? How come you guys never
        trust me?

We don't say much, cause it's kinda true. It would be
funny to hear him brag about the experience, but
we'd never know if it really happened or not, which
is mandatory when money's involved. Tobiah says to
take Saul with him to witness and to increase his
chances. Eli gets all pissed off, saying he doesn't need
Saul screwing things up, which made Saul feel pretty
bad. Saul is better looking, and I think Eli's kinda
bitter about it.

Jesus says, "I'll go with you, Eli." To our amazement,
Eli says okay, so he must have been having some
doubts, despite his big talk.

They saunter down the street, and Tobiah says we
should watch from a roof. So we start looking around
for a way to get up on the string of buildings that
lead over to where the prostitutes are. We find a
relatively low roof,
but nothing to climb up on. So Tobiah tells Oren to
stand against the wall, and he climbs up
Oren. Saul and I do the same, but Oren is too heavy
for us to lift up, so he says he'll stay put.

We sneak across the roofs, and just as we get close to
where Eli and Jesus are talking to these two
prostitutes, all of a sudden Saul falls through one of
the crappy roofs. He's sticking up about waste high,
so we try to pull him back up, right after we hear this

woman scream. Apparently, there was a couple in the throes of passion, shall we say, and Saul's legs were dangling over them. So the guy grabs Saul's legs and starts pulling, yelling at the top of his lungs. After a tug of war using Saul as the rope (his scared face – seriously, it was *classic*), the guy finally wins, and Saul disappears down the hole. Tobiah and I watch from above as Saul runs around the room, trying to get away from this big guy who wants to inflict some serious harm on him for interrupting his pleasure. Tobiah and I yell at him to "run out the door," and finally Saul does just that, as we high-tail it off the roof, practically landing on Oren as he tries to help us down.

We peek into the street and Saul is hauling ass down the street so fast that he loses a sandal. So the three of us calmly walk into the big guy's way, and he barrels into us, knocking us all down, and just keeps going. Just then, Eli and Jesus show up with these two prostitutes who all want to know what the hubbub is about. Tobiah and I start telling the story, taking turns, and everyone starts laughing and pretty soon we're all kind of hanging out together.

The big guy comes storming back, so we figure he never caught up with Saul. He sees us and yells at us for being too young to be on the street, and that we should run back to our mommies like our friend did, and that the girls shouldn't bother with us cause we don't have any money and we're too young to have dicks.

We kind of shuffled off, because a bunch of people were looking at us from windows and doorways and we felt pretty stupid. So Jesus invites the girls to come back with us to hang out at his house. My jaw literally dropped about a foot. And they said yes! I gotta say, Jesus really surprised me with having the balls to even ask.

I had always wondered what prostitutes look like. They have really long hair, which is pretty hot. They aren't as attractive as I'd imagined, though. The short one had some jaggedy teeth, so she always held her hand over her mouth. But by the end of the evening, her teeth didn't look as bad. Must have been the light or something. She was the one Jesus talked to, like the whole night.

We found Saul hiding behind the temple. He told us the whole story again from his perspective, and it was freakin' hilarious.

Jesus' folks have a little courtyard in front of their house with chairs built by Jesus' dad, so we all sat around and talked and laughed.
Jesus' mom came out, but she's pretty cool, and just told us all not to be too loud. I don't know, maybe she didn't realize who the girls were. The taller one sat next to Saul, which I'm sure pissed off Eli, so Eli sat on the other side of her. He tried putting his arm around her at one point, but she pushed it off. Eli joked about it, saying, "I know you don't want to let the others know I'm your favorite, but that's alright, I understand."

Finally, Jesus' mom came out again and told us it was time to go home. We walked the girls to the end of their street, and said goodnight and walked back. Eli tried teasing Jesus about spending so much time with the short one, but he just did that smile of his. Tobiah said, "Oh, by the way, Eli, you need to pay us all, since you didn't win the bet."

Eli got a scared look on his face, like he'd forgotten about the bet, and now he'd have to pay up. But then Jesus said, "well, he did spend the evening with two prostitutes for free. And we even got to join him. I'd say we're all even."

Tobiah was mad that he didn't get to collect from Eli, whose nickname should be "cheap bastard." It would have been sweet revenge. He said, "Jesus, you weren't even in on the bet, you don't get a say in this."

Oren said, "I don't know – it makes sense to me. Jesus is right."

Tobiah finally gave in, but he wasn't happy about it. Saul grabbed him in a friendly headlock and started walking him home. "Come on, Tobes, time to hit the hay."

As Oren and I headed off, I heard Eli say to Jesus, "I owe you one, man." He didn't answer, but I'll just bet he gave Eli one of his creepy smiles.

1:3

Eli's dad, Tehvah, is a very prosperous sandal maker here in Nazareth. So Eli never really has to work very hard, and he usually spends his money on trying to "look good for the ladies." If you ask me, the entire Roman Empire doesn't have enough money to make *that* work.

About a month ago, Tehvah decides that Eli is getting too lazy and too skinny, and he needs to do some real work. So he gives Eli the job of chopping wood, and since Eli *is* lazy and skinny, he somehow conned me into chopping with him. I guess I finally agreed because a few more muscles wouldn't hurt my chances with the ladies, either. And, well, he is my friend.

Funny thing is, we wound up having this really good talk about stuff. Eli can be a first class dick, but he's also a good guy, and pretty great if you can get him to talk about something other than himself and girls. He loves his folks, cares a lot about our gang of guys, and might actually be a good husband and father if he'll ever drop his cool guy act and find a girl who's crazy enough to marry him.

Seems like marriage has been on our collective minds a good deal lately. Not that we talk about it much. But I've noticed Oren talking quietly to Leah when no one else is looking. She's pretty shy, too. And I think Tobiah likes Shayna: she's pretty, but not very bright. You'd think a smart guy like Tobiah would want some sort of intellectual equal, but I guess he really likes being the expert.

Saul – well, *all* the girls like Saul. He's a nice guy and nice looking, too. Like Shayna, he's not the brightest, and I think that gets all the girls feeling all maternal towards him. It must be hard for him to think about who he'd want, given he could have his pick.

Me, I don't want to marry a girl from Nazareth. I want to marry a city girl and have a life where there's lots going on, and we'll have a bunch of kids running all over the place. The other guys probably think I'm not interested in girls cause I'm not falling all over myself with any of the local talent. But I know what I'm looking for, and I'm sure that when I find her, I'll be falling all over myself, too. The trouble is, how to meet a city girl if I never go to a city?

I have no idea what girls look for in a guy. Looks, I guess. I think I'm okay in that department. Nobody screams when I walk into a room.

There was this one time when Hannah's cousin Martha was out here visiting from Irbid. Man, was she hot. And I mean, knock down, smack your face, *hot*. All the guys were sniffing around her like a pack of wolves. Even Saul got all drooly. Martha was very cool, though; obviously used to the attention. Irbid isn't exactly a city, but I liked the fact that she'd traveled to Nazareth. Shows some spunk. I have to admit, I did a little sniffing of my own.

So once again we're hanging out after dinner, and Eli wants to go over to Hannah's and see if she and Martha will hang out with us. It's funny, cause we were all kind of nervous about it, but in a little while we're pushing each other up to knock on their door. Finally Eli steps up, trying to protect his reputation, and knocks. Hannah's dad comes to the door, and since he knows us pretty well he acts all serious and wants to know what a bunch of hooligans like us want.

Eli says, loading it on pretty heavy: "Good evening, sir. We were wondering if we could trouble you to inform the young ladies of the house that we are offering to take them on a tour of Nazareth, providing commentary on the social, economic and historical aspects of our fair town." Hannah's dad just starts laughing. "Wait here" he says, and closes the door.

We all got excited and Saul starts jumping up and down. "Dude, be cool!" his brother tells him.

Hannah and Martha come out all smiley and shy, and her dad says, "I trust you fine young hooligans will be careful with my girls and bring them back well before sunset?"

We promise we will and head off. So we're walking along and Martha just blurts out, "Is there a place to go swimming? In Irbid, that's what my friends and I do."

Okay. Imagine the sound of six erections firing up simultaneously. Cause that's what happened next. And maybe there was no audible sound, but to us, it was like the Roman Legion marching into town with their trumpets and drums and… well, you get the idea. The thought of hot Martha, wet and naked, would do that to a blind man.

We try to get more info on just who her friends are – guys and girls, or just girls, or what? – but she plays it cool. Hannah just giggles.

Down by the river, we all just kind of stand there. It's a really nice summer evening, warm with a slight breeze, the early evening sun shining sideways through the palms. Martha says she and Hannah will go behind some trees and meet us farther down river, and they disappear in the brush.

We just kind of look at each other, like, so does that mean… ? What *does* that mean?

Eli says, "You guys are a bunch of babies," and pulls off his clothes and slides into the water. Saul starts giggling, and Tobiah starts walking back to town. Jesus says, "C,mon, let's do this thing," but I heard a little crack in his voice. I figured, what the hell. So I joined in as we start pulling off our clothes, Saul giggling the whole time. Oren groans with indecision and starts stripping down.

We waded down the river, with the water about waist high. Since it was summer, there was barely any current. We waited for a while, then Oren started splashing me, so I got him back, and we all got into this splashing war, sort of forgetting to stay low in the water. Then we heard the girls laughing.

Hannah and Martha were standing on a rise, fully clothed, looking down at us. We all kind of slunk down in the water, except for Eli who stands up spread eagle and lets out a big whoop. The girls ran off laughing. We'd been *had*: big time. All of a sudden, Oren says, "our clothes!" We rushed back to where we'd left them. Not too surprisingly, they were all gone. Only our sandals were left.

Saul's eyes looked like they were about to pop out of his head. "What are we supposed to do *now*?" Jesus strategically held his sandals in front and behind. "How's this?" he said. Eli was kinda mad about it. He didn't mind being seen
in the river, but was ticked off about having to humiliate ourselves in front of the whole town. Honestly, I was quietly freaking out. Oren said we should draw straws to see who should go back into town to get clothes for the rest of us, but none of us was too keen on that idea. We heard someone coming down the path, so we slid back into the water.

As luck would have it, it was Tobiah, carrying our clothes. He'd figured out their game as he was walking back to town (smart guy that he is) and when he was walking back to warn us, he ran into the girls and told them to give him the clothes back.

They'd just dropped them and walked off, all superior. Stupid girls.

Martha was still in town for a couple more weeks, but Eli was the only one who was willing to look her in the eye. Usually winking at her. That guy.

1:4

Jesus, man. I am so fucking pissed at him right now. For someone who professes to be my friend, he has become such a betrayer.

Okay, so Roman soldiers march through Nazareth every once in a while, and it gets everyone kind of stirred up. Usually they're just marching from Point A to Point B, and couldn't care less about our boring little town. This one
day it was late afternoon when they tromped through, and it was hot as hell. We were all walking home from school when we saw them stopped at the well, filling their water bags and watering the officers' horses.

They were a pretty scrappy looking bunch. You'd think Roman soldiers would be all regal and stuff, but they looked tired, dirty and pissed. So we just stood there and watched them.

One of the guys looked pretty young, like just a couple of years older than us. Tobiah wondered what he was doing way out here. Most of the soldiers we saw were the older career soldiers who were grizzled like burnt meat. And the officers were old, too. We guessed they were sent here as a punishment for something. Eli said they were all greedy bastards, and Jesus said he felt sorry for them marching all over the countryside in capes and helmets and armor and all in this heat. Which almost started a fight between them.

But then the young soldier walks over to this old lady who sells eggs, takes an egg, cracks it, sucks it down, throws the shell at her feet and walks away. When she said he needed to pay, he just laughed and said something in Italian that made the other soldiers laugh, too. So then a couple of other soldiers walked over and did the same thing. And she's just this nice old lady; never did anyone any harm.

I don't know where I got the idea (or the balls), but I walked over to the old lady, paid for an egg, and hustled along a shortcut through the thicket, down the road, and hid in the bushes. All the guys (except for Jesus) showed up a few minutes later, but I wouldn't say a word to them.

Eli: What is up with you?
Oren: Don't do something stupid.
Tobiah: There are plenty of other options here.
Saul: What's he doing? Why isn't he saying anything?

Tobiah: Saul, please.
Saul: What?
Eli: Would you guys shut up?
Oren: Shhhh! Here they come.

We could hear the troop marching from about half a mile away. Two officers on horseback, and about a dozen soldiers marching miserably behind. As they got closer, I could feel a jangling in my arm and the hair on the back of my neck started moving around. Just as they passed us, I popped up and pegged the young soldier with the egg, right on the back of his helmet. Perfect shot.

The guy stopped marching and turned around, which made all the soldiers behind him slam into each other - classic. One officer yelled at them, and the head guy *really* yelled at them.

The young soldier tried to explain, but the first officer started smacking him with this big stick-thing, like a cudgel. You could tell the young guy thought about hitting back, but he knew better. Some of the other soldiers were looking around to see who'd done it, but they couldn't see us. The head guy turned and started riding off, so the officer yelled again and they started marching.

I'm not sure what I thought would happen to me, but I didn't care. I guess I could have been whipped or killed or something. What that punk soldier did was wrong. You don't treat old people like that, I don't care who you are. So Eli and Oren thought it turned out pretty cool, but the twins were worried that somehow they'd track me down.

Well, it came pretty close to that. Saul told Jesus about it, and that night, he kind of pulls me aside. What pissed me off is that he started off sounding like he was on my side.

"So how did that feel, hitting him right on the helmet?" Jesus asked. "Nice shot, by the way."
"It felt awesome," I told him. "I'd do it again in a heartbeat."
"How do you think the soldier felt?"
"Pissed! He'll think again before he treats another Nazarene like that."

Jesus kind of stooped down and started drawing something in the dirt. Really quietly, without looking at me, he says, "And how would you feel if you had to serve as a soldier because you couldn't afford a better life, and
were sent hundreds of miles away from your home and felt like a stranger and an outcast,
and you'd been marching in the heat for years and you just wanted something to give you the strength to get you through another pointless march through some god-forsaken country, and some unknown person nails you with an egg as an insult, without having the guts to face you? How do you think you'd feel then?"

I must have had smoke coming out of my ears or something, cause Oren saw us and could tell something was wrong with me. He told me later he'd never seen anybody look so red and tight. "Hey, are you okay?" he asked me.

No. I wasn't. I wanted to kick Jesus in the face; smash that self-righteous prick face down in his little dirt drawings and ask him how *that* felt. So I walked away, and that just made me madder. I started to walk back towards that bastard, and Oren stepped in front of me. "Hey, hey, take it easy. What did he say to you?" I just shook my head. I started towards Jesus again, and Oren really held me. "C'mon," he said, "let's go for a walk." By that time, all the other guys could tell something was going on, and as Oren and I walked away, I could hear them questioning Jesus. Didn't hear what he said, though.

It's been a few days, and I still haven't talked to Jesus. I *refuse* to. He's kept his distance, not just from me, but from the whole group. Good riddance, I say. He was never one of us anyway, always going off by himself to figure out the fucking universe or something.

I haven't slept much lately, either. Which just makes me grumpier. I keep thinking about what he said, and how I should have decked the fucker right there. I was madder at him than I was at the soldier. What he said actually made me pity the soldier a little bit, but I couldn't even look at Jesus.

Thing is, Jesus is pretty strong from his carpentry work, so he could probably beat the crap out of me if he wanted. Not that I've ever seen him hurt even a fly. Then I go back and forth if it was a smart thing to back off or not. My dad says to just let it go. That in another few weeks I'll have forgotten why I was so mad, but I don't think so.

And it's not even like I want to get revenge on him. I just want him to go away. Forever.

I fucking hate him.

1:5

It's been ten days since I talked to Jesus, and I can't say I'm feeling much better. He hasn't hung around with us, either.

So, the rest of us are hanging out down by the river, and it's pretty quiet, like everybody is waiting for something. All of a sudden, Saul
says he thinks we should let Jesus back in. He looks at me as he says it, but everyone else is looking somewhere else. I guess they all knew it was coming. I gotta give him credit for speaking his mind on his own. He's usually more of a follower.

Me: Why are you looking at me, I never said he
     couldn't hang out with us.

Saul: Well, no, I guess not.

Eli: He only hangs with us when he wants, anyway. Nobody's stopping him.

Saul: C'mon guys, you know what I mean. I like having him around, and all this tension isn't fun. Can we just get back to normal?"

Tobiah: Yeah, I have to agree. Enough is enough. It's so tense around here. We haven't laughed in a long time.

Saul: So, is it okay, Joel? Can I tell him he's welcome again?

I have to tell you, I really did think about it. But then I remembered that feeling when he betrayed me, and I got sick to my stomach again. "Fine, he can join you." I said calmly. "I guess I'll see you guys later."

Oren finally spoke up. "Joel, you have to forgive him sometime."

"Really?" I asked him. "I *have* to?"

Silence.

"Look," I said, "you guys hang out with him all you want. I just don't want to be around when you do."

Saul lets out this groan. Again, pretty surprising for him. "Please, Joel."

"Why?" I ask him.

"I don't know. Because it's the right thing to do?"

"Not for me."

"Well, then, do it for me. We're friends, right? Please?"

Oh, man. Leave it to Saul to stumble on the one argument I couldn't deny. Tobiah may have gotten the smarts and Saul the looks, but Saul also has quite a bit of heart. And I could tell this was really bothering him, or he wouldn't have spoken up.

He was standing there looking at me with eyes pleading for acceptance, like a stray dog. As I've said before, Saul is like our collective little brother, and it was hard to turn my back on him. It was so heartfelt, I felt like a jerk letting him down. So yeah, I caved. Believe me, you would have, too. But it was for my friend Saul, and *not* Jesus. So maybe that's okay.

Saul had given up and was turning away with his head down, when I said, "Okay, you win." "*Really*?" Saul asked, as if he could hardly believe it. "Yeah. Really."

The other guys all said stuff like, "that's more like it," and "yeah, man," and they patted Saul on the back. I think they were afraid to deal with me directly, in case I changed my mind. We all started walking back to town, and Saul hung back to give me this look, one of real appreciation. It somehow made me feel a lot better.

We walked for a while in silence while the other guys joked around ahead of us. I put my hand on Saul's shoulder and said, "Only for you, Saul. Because you *are* my friend." He kept looking down, but I could see he had a huge smile on his face. Then he yelled up to his brother, "Tobiah, where are those dates you bought today? Can I have one?"

Tobiah sighed. "Saul," he said,"remember that talk we had about keeping some things secret?" Sure enough, once we all knew he had dates, we all wanted some and pretty soon they were all gone.

That night, Jesus saw us at the well, so he came up, and everyone was pretty cool and generally friendly. Maybe they were worried that I'd blow my top again, but I didn't. I just stayed kind of quiet. And it actually felt okay.

I slept pretty well that night. First time in ten days.

1:6

So we're strolling around town after dinner, and we happened to walk by Jesus' house. He was sitting on his front step, whittling this little block of wood. When we walked up and he showed it to us, it was this bird. Like a really good carved bird. And Oren says, "Can you show me how to do that?"

Next thing you know, we're all drifting through his dad's shop, looking for chunks of wood laying around. I find one, but immediately get a big nasty splinter in my thumb. Jesus comes right over when he hears me swear, and says, "those are no big deal – I get them all the time." He somehow pulls the splinter out with his fingernails and then rubs his thumb over the wound. "There," he says, "you're all set."

I looked down at it, and sure enough, it looked like it had never been touched. Not even a drop of blood.
"Hey," I say. "What did you just do?"
"It's a carpenter's trick," he says.
All the other guys started hitting him up with questions about their block of wood and what could they make out of it, so I let it go.

Jesus found tools for all of us, so we're sitting around his front courtyard in a circle, each of us trying to coax some animal out of the wood. Oren was shaping out a lion, Eli and Tobiah a bull, Saul a monkey. I was trying to see a dog in
mine. It was slow going at first, as we all got used to the tools. Then Eli scrapes his hand with an awl, and blood starts oozing out. Jesus takes him inside to wash it off and put a bandage on it. They come back out after a few minutes and no bandage. Oren says, "hey, how's your hand?"

"Good," says Eli, and he holds it up. Not a scratch.

"What the...?" I say.

Tobiah says, "Jesus, let me see your hands." He holds them out, and they're rough but there's only one big scar on his left hand.

Tobiah says, "Where did that come from?" meaning the scar.

Jesus says, "That was when the lion got me."

"Bullshit" says Eli.

Saul laughs, "There aren't any lions around here."

Jesus says, "Not around here – in Egypt."

Tobiah, looks at him with his head cocked to one side. "You sticking with that story?"

Jesus says, "When I was young, my family lived in Egypt."

At that moment, Oren accidently jabs himself in the leg. "Blistering buck!" he yells out.

Jesus sighs. "C'mon, let's get that cleaned up."

Tobiah hustles after them: "I wanna see this." Jesus puts out his hand, "just wait here. It'll be your turn soon enough."

When Oren and Jesus came back out, there was still a rip in Oren's robe and a little blood stain, but his leg was fine. Jesus' dad came out, too, and went around collecting all the tools from us.

Jesus was like, "No, Dad, wait, it's okay."

"No, it's not okay," his dad said. "If you boys aren't properly trained on how to use these tools, you can do a lot of damage to yourself."

"But Dad…"

"No, Jesus. No." He said it like he was expecting an argument. "It's not just about the tools. We've talked about this." Then he walked to the workroom. Jesus' folks seemed pretty cool, but there was also kind of a funny tension, too. Jesus was clearly put out by his dad's paranoia, but he just took it. "Sorry, guys."

Tobiah said, "Forget about the carving, what is going on with the instant healing?"

Saul chimed in, "Can you teach us how to do *that*?"

"Can't really talk about that."

Tobiah said, "why not?"

"I'm not supposed to. Yet."

We all kind of looked at each other like, WTF? *So* weird.

Finally, Oren says to Eli, "Dude, that doesn't look anything like a bull."

"I wasn't done yet," says Eli. "Is that supposed to be a lion?"

"It IS a lion."

"Where's the mane?"

"Right there."

"I thought that was his butt."

"Why would a lion have such a big butt?"

"How the hell should I know, I've never seen one. Have you?"

"I've seen pictures."

"Did they have a big butt?"

"No!"

"Then why does yours?"

"It doesn't!" Oren turned to Jesus, "Jesus, does this look like a lion?"

"I don't know. Where's the mane?"

"RIGHT THERE!"

Saul and I started laughing at that point. Tobiah just shook his head and said, "For I will be unto Ephraim as a lion, and as a big assed lion to the house of Judah."

After the buzz-kill, we weren't so excited about the carving anymore, so we decided to sacrifice our various carved animals to God. We didn't want to let Jesus cause his bird was so good, but he said all such things must come to dust, or something like that, and he threw it in the funeral pyre with the dog, monkey, two bulls and the big-assed lion.

I hope He liked them.

1:7

Ezra the basket-weaver's son has a thing for Saul. Which is okay, I guess, but since Saul isn't into guys, it makes him pretty uncomfortable. Maybe he's a little flattered, but I don't know.

Well late one night, we're walking around town after our usual hijinks, and we hear this crying behind the temple. So we go check it out. And it's Ezra, all curled up in a ball.

"Dude," says Eli, "What's up, man? You're crying like a girl." Not the most sensitive guy in the world. Ezra: Go away.
Oren: C'mon, you don't want to be out here this late. We'll walk you home.
Ezra doesn't say anything.
Eli: Let's go, buddy. It's late, we gotta get home, and we're not leaving you here. Let's go!

Sensitivity up one notch.

So Ezra stands up, and he's got bruises, blood under his nose and a big shiner of a black eye.
Eli: Dude, what happened to you?
Ezra: What does it look like?
Saul: It looks like somebody beat the crap out of you.
Oren: I hope you got him good, too.
Ezra: It wasn't a him, it was a them.
Oren: Who was it?
Ezra doesn't answer. "C'mon," says Oren.

We started walking and didn't say much else. We could guess who had done it. We were never, like, friends with Ezra, but we all felt bad that he'd been beat up.

Then Saul said, "Hey, let's see if Jesus can fix him up."
Ezra's guard went up. "What does that mean?"
"You know," Saul said to the rest of us, "how he heals stuff?"
It was a good idea. So we headed over to Jesus' house.

It was pretty clear that they had all gone to bed. We told Tobiah he had to go wake up Jesus because he was the smartest of the bunch of us, and therefore the most respected, which meant he'd get in the least amount of trouble if someone else woke up by mistake. So he tiptoed through their yard and tapped ever so lightly on the shutter. Jesus suddenly came around the corner and put his hand on Tobiah's shoulder to let him know he was there. Tobiah jumped about eight feet in the air. We all started laughing but tried to keep quiet, which just made it worse. Even Ezra smiled a bit.

We all made our way to an open field, still stifling our laughs, Ezra kind of hanging back. Oren finally spoke up and said, "Jesus, Ezra got worked over tonight, and we thought maybe you could, you know, do your 'carpenter thing' like you did the other day."

Jesus nodded, sighed, and led Ezra a little ways away and spoke to him just softly enough so we couldn't hear what he was saying. Tobiah was watching intently, being the one most interested in this whole crazy Jesus talent. Oren was like, "Dude, don't stare."

Tobiah: I want to see what he does.
Saul: I feel bad for the guy. I don't know what I'd do if I didn't have you guys to watch my back.
Eli: Okay, no. We're not adopting him.
Oren: Adopting him? What are you talking about? He's not a puppy or something.
Eli: Yeah, but Saul's feeling all sorry for him. Now he's gonna get all mushy and fall in love with him.
Tobiah: Sounds like you're jealous, Eli.
Eli fired back with the classic, "shut the hell up."

I finally spoke up. "Maybe we *should* adopt him. I mean, like, as a friend. The guy hasn't had any friends since forever, and maybe those assholes would think twice about beating him up."

Eli: I do not like where this is going.
Tobiah kept his eyes glued on Jesus and Ezra,
and said, "maybe he got what he deserved. I mean,
why would a guy like guys? It's not normal."
Me: It doesn't matter what he likes or dislikes,
it's not cool to gang up on someone and beat the crap
out of him when he's alone.
Oren: And he's pretty much always alone.

I was kinda surprised how loudly I was talking. I
wasn't sure where it was coming from, since I
had never given Ezra a second thought before. I
just know I don't like bullies. Like the whole Roman
soldier incident.

Eli: Even if it means he hangs with us *all the
        time*?
Me: Even if it means he hangs with us all the
time.
Oren: Tobiah, what if it was Saul that got beat
up? How would you feel then? I'd be okay hanging
out with Ezra if it meant he never gets beat up again.
Tobiah: Saul, are you cool with that?
Saul: Well, yeah. I mean, as long as he doesn't try to
kiss me or something.
Tobiah: What if he did?

"I'd beat the cra…" Saul started, but caught himself.
"Oh, man."

Jesus and Ezra came back, and I have to say, Ezra

was looking a hell of lot better. Oren said, "How're you feeling?"

Ezra took a deep breath. "Better. But I think I'd like to go home now."

Jesus said, "We'll walk you home. But I think they have something to say to you."

What? How could he have heard what we were saying?

Saul launched right in. "You should hang with us. Seriously."

Ezra looked stunned. "Really? You mean it?" We all nodded, even Eli.

Saul added, "Just don't, like, kiss me or anything."

Ezra smiled. "Okay. It's a deal."

Oren put in, "But if you *have* to kiss somebody, go for Eli."

Eli started for Oren with fists clenched, but not before Oren dodged behind Jesus, then high-tailed it off into the field. We could hear Oren laughing and Eli yelling, "You can't run forever!" and Oren answering from far away, "Watch me!"

And that's how it happened that Ezra become one of us.

1:8

So now that we've been true to our word and have been hanging out with Ezra for a while now, he invited the six of us over to dinner one night to thank us.

I have to say, Ezra is pretty cool. He's definitely shy, which is no surprise after the way he's been treated – even by us. A few people started making stupid comments about all of us liking guys, too, but we didn't care. We figured they were jealous that Ezra joined us, when *they* really wanted to. I mean, honestly, we are like the coolest guys in town. Seriously, I'm not just saying that. Whatever.

Today before the dinner, Eli started getting all, "I'm not sure if I want to go," so we just reminded him that we had decided this as a group, and then we threatened to kick his ass. He got all huffy, but we didn't care. I'd seen him joking around with Ezra the other day in spite of himself, so I knew he was just being weird.

And speaking of weird and/or annoying, Jesus decides to make Ezra one of his carved birds to give him when we arrive. Damn. Now the rest of us will look like a bunch of lame-os.

So we all meet at the well and walk down towards Ezra's. We pass through his dad's shop while all the hanging baskets bump against our heads. The door is open and his folks are scurrying around getting things ready. As soon as they see us, his mother yells out "Ezraaaaaa!", and his dad hustles into the kitchen without even saying hello. As we file in, his mom just stands there and smiles at us, her eyes starting to water. Then she scurries off, too. Funny.

We look at the table and there is a *ton* of food, and it all looks and smells really good. His mom pops her head out; "Ezra made all of it, I only helped a little!"

Ezra comes out all sheepish. "Hey, guys. Welcome, welcome."
Jesus steps forward and hands him his damn carved bird. Ezra is clearly impressed. "It's beautiful. You made this?"
Jesus says, "Yes. I'm glad you like it."
Eli says, "It's from all of us." Which is kind of a crappy thing to do, but I wish I'd thought of it.
Ezra smiles and says, "Dinner is ready, so let's eat!"

Oh, man – it was truly an impressive spread; chickpea soup, brisket, lamb stew, grilled fish with pomegranate sauce, honey glazed carrots, rice and fresh bread. Everything tasted better than the last thing until you went back and tasted the first thing again. Then we had an apple nut cake and figs for dessert.

Oren: Oh, my stomach hurts, but I am *so* happy right now.
Tobiah: Eli, seriously, *another* piece of cake? Are you hollow?

Eli: I want to fff… (*a quick glance towards the kitchen*) …*marry* this cake.

Tobiah: What about Rachel, your true love?

Jesus: Considering how he's been doing with her, the cake may be a better option.

Me: Whoa. One for Jesus!

Eli: I'm so in love, I don't care what you say.

Saul: Mhhff mweffm hmm….

Ezra: I'm sorry what was that?

Saul: (*finishes chewing*) How did you learn to cook like this?

Ezra: Umm, let's just say I've had a lot of free time. What did you guys like best?

Eli: CAAAAAKE!

Saul: CAAAAAKE!

Tobiah: The lamb stew. I could eat that every single day for the rest of my entire life.

Jesus: I can't get enough of the bread and fish.

Oren: Maybe one more bowl of soup.

Tobiah: You've already had dessert.

Oren: It calls to me.

Ezra: Go ahead, there's still some left.

Eli: Dude, taking you in was like the best thing we ever did.

Oren: Totally.

Jesus: Verily.

Tobiah: You got that right.

Saul: CAAAAAKE!

Ezra: Yeah, well, this was my big thank you. But I'm not doing this all the time.

Eli: What, we aren't doing this every week?

Tobiah: He's joking.

Ezra: I'll cook, but you guys have to pay for it.

Oren: Ah, the only magic words to discourage Eli. You're learning fast, Ezra.

Eli: Shut up, Oren.

Saul: Man, any girl would be lucky to marry a good cook like you.

Awkward.

Tobiah: Saul?

Saul: Oh, right. Sorry.

Ezra: It's okay. I'm glad you're enjoying it. And I like you guys. I really do. I was a little worried at first. Like maybe it was a trap or something. So, thanks for being… dare I say it?... my friends.

Oren: Hey, it's been good having you around, Ezra.

Saul: Yeah.

Eli: CAAAAKE!

Everyone: CAAAAAKE!

Tobiah: Those bruises sure healed fast. What exactly do you do, Jesus?

Jesus: Some people cook. I heal. (*insert creepy smile*)

Tobiah: And you're not going to tell us how?

Jesus: Would a good cook give out his best recipe? Or his secret ingredient?

Ezra: I already know what the secret ingredient is to both.

Tobiah: What?

Ezra: Can I tell them, Jesus?

Jesus: Sure.

Ezra: Love.

Eli: Oh, please. That is so sappy.

Oren: This from the guy who wants to marry a cake.

We had pretty much finished off everything, so we decided to go for a walk. Once we were out of earshot of most people, we started belching. Eli started us off with a roar like a bull in heat.

Tobiah went, "tsk, tsk, Eli."
Eli said, "what, it's a compliment on the meal!"
Jesus said, "and that was from all of us."
We all laughed at that.

Then the competitive farting started. It was a very satisfying evening.

1:9

Now I'm not one to eavesdrop, but the weirdest thing happened last week. Two times I happened to overhear some pretty juicy conversations. And it wasn't my fault, I swear.

We'd all been hanging out by the river and walked back into town just as it started getting dark. Apparently Eli had been sitting on an anthill and some ants had gotten into his underwear and all of a sudden I guess they realized where they were and weren't too happy about it. I don't blame them.

We happened to be walking by the temple, when he goes, "what the… ? Ants!" and starts dancing around, trying to get them out. We're all laughing at him cause he's so gangly and not a good dancer anyway. He realizes we're out in public and decides to duck behind the temple to lose the ants. He's back in the dark dancing away with his robe lifted up, trying to shake out the ants. I happened to see a bucket of water sitting there, so I went over to give it to him so he could wash them away with one splash. Well, just before I got to him, the Rabbi comes out of the temple with a little lantern and sees Eli, but his back was to me, so I ducked behind a pillar.

"Young man," the Rabbi yells, "what are you doing!?!"
Eli looked up and froze. "What does it look like?" as if the answer was obvious.
"Eli, is that you?" asked the Rabbi. "Oh Eli, Eli. How could you desecrate yourself like that - and behind the temple! You should be ashamed of yourself!"
Eli, still confused, says "what? Oh. No! No, no, no, I was just shaking the ants out of my pants."
The Rabbi, shaking his head says, "oh, my son, I don't know what you kids call it these days, but you should never touch yourself like that. Are you so lonely?"
"Rabbi, I swear, I wasn't… doing that."
"It's all right, Eli. We have all been young and foolish. But you mustn't do such things. What would your parents say? "
"Oh please, no, don't tell them I…"
"Don't worry, your secret is safe with me. Just promise me you won't do this again. Such things are for you and a wife. You do want to get married someday don't you?"
"Rabbi, listen to me, I wasn't…"

"Eli, promise me. You have your whole life before you, and Yahweh forbid you should be smote for such deviance."

"But I wasn't… oh, all right, I promise. Just go back to… whatever it is you guys do."

The Rabbi stood for a moment shaking his finger at Eli, and then shuffled back into the temple.
I stepped out of the shadows and Eli said, "What the hell was that?"

I was cracking up. I tried to tell him I'd brought the water for him, but I could hardly breathe.
When the other guys came over, wondering what was taking so long, I laughed so hard
trying to tell them what happened, I dropped the bucket.

Oren said, "Eli, what did you do to Joel? He's gone crazy."
Eli said, "Nothing! Why is everyone accusing me of things I didn't do?"

Once the story got out, Eli got more and more pissed off, but we were all laughing. "I don't *do* that!" he kept saying. "I don't *need* to do that."
Tobiah was like, "sure, sure; none of *us* have ever stroked the snake."
Oren: Shucked the corn.
Saul: Yanked the cord.
Ezra: Polished the sword.
Me: Buffed the banana.
Eli: Well *you* guys might have, but I'm a player.

Saul said, "Eli, this is what you looked like," and he went into this crazy dance that got us all laughing again. It was so funny, even Eli had to laugh – after he had Saul in a headlock.

We finally started going our separate ways back to our respective houses. Ezra kind of pulled Jesus aside and said he wanted to talk to him about something, and they wandered off.

One thing I like to do is climb trees. Not all the time, just when I feel like it. So after everybody had taken off, I climbed this tree to just enjoy the evening and watch the night grow dark. After a few minutes, there was no one around and Jesus and Ezra happened to walk back under my tree. And stop. So I listened.

Jesus: So, Ezra, we never got around to what you wanted to talk about.
Ezra: Well, it's sort of about you. And me. See, I feel like you've become a really important person in my life.
Jesus: Thank you, Ezra.
Ezra: And I wonder how you feel about me.
Jesus: Umm, I think you're a good guy. But, um,…
Ezra: Jesus, you are such a loving man. Not to mention really muscular. And you've given me a whole new feeling about myself and life.
Jesus: I'm glad.
Ezra: In fact, I can't imagine my life without you. (*he starts getting choked up*).

Jesus: Oh, hey, Ezra, c'mon. You've always had everything you need. I think you're giving me too much credit.

Ezra: Can I hug you?

Jesus: Umm, sure.

They hugged. And it was like a long time gramma hug. So long, that you start thinking about what you're going to have for breakfast the next day. Finally Jesus backed away.

Jesus: Okay, Ezra.

Ezra: When you said that love was the main ingredient…

Jesus: I think *you* actually said that.

Ezra: … it just meant so much to me.

Jesus: Ezra, I'm not what you're looking for. It's the sense of peace you want, and that doesn't come from me.

Ezra: Where does it come from?

Jesus: My Father.

Ezra: I've never even met your father.

Jesus: No, not *that* father, *our* Father. Who's in heaven?

Ezra: Oh. Really?

Jesus: Yes, really. I'm sorry if you were confused.

Ezra: You sound really sure about this.

Jesus: I am. Believe me, I am.

Ezra: Okay. I guess.

Jesus: I thought you kinda liked Saul?

Ezra: Hmm. Really nice guy. Just not all that bright.

Jesus: He's a good friend, yes?

Ezra: Yes. He is.

Jesus: You have six good friends now. The rest will come in time.

Ezra: Don't you want to find someone?

Jesus: Yeah, sure. But I don't know if I ever will.

Ezra: Why not?

Jesus lets out a big sigh. "My Dad doesn't like me dating anyone."

Ezra: *Any*one?

Jesus: Pretty much.

Ezra: He sounds pretty strict.

Jesus: You have no idea.

Ezra: Wait, which dad are we talking about now?

Jesus: Actually, they're a lot alike on this subject.

Ezra: Oh. Well, good night, Jesus. If *you* ever need to talk...

Jesus: Thanks.

Ezra headed off, and I had to hand it to Jesus, he got out of that pretty clean. Then I heard him say my name. Damn.

"Joel, I know you're up there."

"How the hell did you know that?" I said as I jumped down. "I didn't make a sound."

"Have you forgiven me about the Roman soldier thing?" he asked me.

Whoa – where did that come from?

"Maybe. I guess," I said. "Why?"

"Because I don't want there to be any bad blood between us."

"So you're not exactly apologizing."

"No. No, I'm not. Would that help?"

"It wouldn't hurt."

"Look, we're all learning and growing. Maybe I didn't say it right, but I think you got what I was trying to say – even if it was hard to hear."

"Yeah. Yeah, okay. So was that the apology?" I smiled.

"Sure. "He smiled back, but not the creepy smile. "Your turn."

I stopped smiling. "Okay, here's the deal. I don't really understand you, and sometimes you weird me out. I guess you mean well, but like you said, your delivery needs some serious work."

"Noted. Thanks. I'm overcome with emotion from that touching apology."

"Jerk," I called him.

"Numbskull," he responded.

 "Freak."

"Dweeb."

"Jackass."

"Hothead."

We slowly walked our separate ways, continuing our verbal volley until we couldn't hear each other anymore.

1:10

Tobiah says, "Jesus. You have to tell me about this healing stuff."
I tag on, "And how you know things without anyone telling you. "

We're out in an open field, lying on our backs and looking up at the stars on yet another quiet night in Nazareth. Not that there's any other kind.
Jesus says, "What do you want to know?"
"How do you do it?" Tobiah says. "Are you like a prophet or something?"
"I can't really explain it."
"No, c'mon on, no more dodging the issue." Tobiah's curiosity had been building for weeks. He'd spent even more time with his religious studies, wondering if this could be some sort of cosmic sign. But how could that be? It was just weird-ass Jesus!

"I think I hear my mom calling me."
Tobiah says, "no, you don't."
"My dad?"
Tobiah says, "no."

Finally Jesus says, "guys, I'd love to talk about it, but it's getting late… "
Tobiah says, "Okay, I'm sorry to have to do this," then he gives us the word: "Get him, now!"
We all grabbed an arm or a leg and held him down. Jesus was pretty casual about it. "Seriously? Even you, Ezra?"

Ezra says, "sorry, Jesus. I'll cook you dinner to make up for it."

Eli jumps to center stage. "You have been dodging our questions forever and ever. No more holding out on us! Tell us now, or… "

Jesus says, "or…?"

Eli says, … we'll, umm… we'll… or… or you'll get the worst pink belly in the history of Nazareth!"

"You guys are really serious about this," says Jesus

Saul yells, "HELL, yes!" And then, "am I hurting you, cause I can ease up a little."

Jesus sighs. "And so it begins. Okay. If I promise to answer all your questions, will you at least let go of me?"

We all nodded agreement, although Tobiah took a while before he did. So we let go and Jesus sits cross-legged on the ground. And he just starts talking. And it just flows out of him, like he's been holding it in for so long, he can't stop it now that it's started. He talks about candles and baskets and hills and lights and fathers and sons and sheep and he's on a fuckin' *roll*! I don't think I can even come close to saying it like he did, so I won't even try. Tobiah started off looking really skeptical, but by the end, he had this look of utter amazement. Ezra even started tearing up. Saul and Oren had this blissful look on their faces and Eli, good old Eli, fell asleep.

Tobiah tried to say something, but it was like he couldn't form the words. Then, suddenly, a snore came out of Eli that could have risen the dead. We all jumped.

Saul burst out with, "Jesus, dude! That was awesome!"
Jesus: So Joel, how was my delivery this time?"
Me: Not bad! Not bad at all. Not sure I got the part about the butter churning.
Jesus: Yeah, I'm thinking about dropping that part.
Me: It sounded vaguely sexual.
Jesus: Hmm, yeah, definitely need to drop that part.
Very slowly, Tobiah said, "So are you like, the One?"
Jesus turned it on him. "What do *you* think?"
Tobiah: I honestly don't know.
Jesus: That kind of answers your question, right?
Oren: Are the stars suddenly brighter, or is it just me?
Saul: That was so righteous! Say it all again!
Jesus: No, I think I'm done for the night.
Tobiah: Waitwaitwait, this is less than settled.
Jesus: How about tomorrow? All that talking kind of took it out of me."
Oren got this sly smile on his face. "Of course, we could give him a pink belly anyway; just for the fun of it."
Jesus was like, "uhh, did you guys hear everything I just said?"
Oren shook Eli awake. We all started to get up but stayed in like, pounce positions.
Jesus said, "guys, it's getting late and… "

We all lunged for him at the same time, just like before, only this time all we grabbed were each other's limbs.

Eli: Oren, let go of me!
Oren: I thought I had Jesus.
Ezra: Oww! Get off of me!
Saul: Sorry, man. Wait, where's Jesus?
Tobiah: He was just here! Where the hell did he go?

Granted, it was dark, but somehow, *somehow*, it was like he vanished. I swear I don't know how he did it. It was definitely no "carpenter's trick." Goosebumps all around.

Eli finally said, "Whoa. What the *hell* just happened?"
Talking in slo-mo, Tobiah said, "hey, you guys don't think… "
Saul: Stop, you're scaring me.
Ezra: But it's Jesus we're talking about, the nice guy we all know and love. There's no need to be afraid. But I think it *is* something.
Tobiah: Personally, I'm pretty confused right now. Maybe this is all a dream.
Saul took that as a cue to punch his brother in the shoulder.
Tobiah yelled, "Saul! What the hell?"
"What, I wanted to see if it was a dream, too."
"By hitting me?"
"I thought that would wake you up!"
"Not if I get punched *in the dream*!"
"I was trying to help you with an answer!"
Oren said, "I nominate Saul as our pink belly substitute."
Saul barely got out the word "guys!" when he was flailing on the ground, getting the worst pink belly in the history of Nazareth.

Part Two

2:1

So maybe you remember last time, Jesus pulled this crazy disappearing act when we were out in the field. He had us all pretty spooked. Who was this guy? We knew he was weird, but this was a whole new level.

Well, it turns out we got even more spooked, cause he really *did* disappear. His parents went around to all of our houses asking if we'd seen him. He'd been missing since that night, and his folks were pretty concerned. They asked all of us what had happened, but we were afraid to tell them. "Well, we were about to give him a pink belly because we wanted to find out if he was a prophet, but he vanished before our eyes. In the dark. In a deserted field. At night." It sounded so crazy, none of us told them anything. Which made us look pretty suspicious. I was starting to get worried that Saul might spill the beans, but fortunately his twin brother Tobiah was there during their questioning, so he covered for him. Plus, I think Saul's stomach still hurt.

We all met together that night. We were worried someone would follow us, so Tobiah said we should just meet at the well, figuring that if we met in plain sight, no one could suspect us of anything. And the crazy thing was we really hadn't *done* anything.

Tobiah: I wonder where Jesus *is*?

Oren: Do you think he disappeared for good?

Ezra: Maybe he's just invisible and he's been here the whole time.

Saul: Don't say scary things like that!

Eli: It's probably just a prank.

Me: Why do I feel guilty?

Oren: Maybe we shouldn't have ganged up on him like that.

Eli: Relax. He'll turn up.

Oren: Do you still think he's a prophet?

Tobiah: Time will tell.

Saul was still kinda creeped out by the idea of invisible Jesus, so he made Tobiah walk him home in the dark. Eli thought the whole thing was kinda silly, so he went home, too. Oren left, so it was just me and Ezra. We were leaning against the well, just shootin' the shit, and Ezra pointed down the street, and said, "wait, is that him?"

I looked, and sure enough, there was Jesus, walking down the road, looking pretty dirty and tired. I don't think I'd ever seen him look so down. We hustled over to him.

"Jesus, are you okay?" Ezra asked.

Jesus stopped, looked at us and smiled. "Yeah, I'm okay. Boy, it's really good to see you guys."

I said, "where have you been? Everybody's been worried about you!"

Jesus said, "everybody?"

"Well, your folks, mostly," I said.

"Oh." Jesus sounded kinda disappointed.

"And us!" Ezra said, smacking me on the arm.

"Where have you been?" I asked.

"Joppa."

"Joppa!? That's like, two days away!" said Ezra, a little too loudly.

"Shh," said Jesus. "I know. I just walked it."

"Hey, how was the beach there?" It just came out of my mouth. I'd always wondered.

Jesus gave me this look. "It was midnight. Wasn't exactly the time to sight see."

"Wait," Ezra said, bringing him over to the well and giving him some water, "so when you vanished you went to Joppa?"

After Jesus drank a bunch of water, he said, "Yeah. Not really where I was aiming for."

"Where *were* you aiming for?" I asked.

"Home!" he said.

He wasn't really up for a lot of questions, and we weren't entirely sure we wanted to know the answers, so we walked him home. His folks were super glad to see him, but kind of hustled him inside and said a quick good night.

The next day Jesus came by my house. It was the first time he'd ever made the effort to see any of us on his own. Usually, he'd just find us hanging out. Frankly, it got me a little nervous.

Me: So, what's up? You feeling better?

Jesus: Yeah. Just wanted to chat a bit about the other night.

Me: I don't suppose you're going to tell me how you got to Joppa?

He gave me this look, like, sheah, right.
Me: So how was the beach?
He laughed.
Me: Maybe you can take us all there sometime?
Jesus: Nah, it doesn't really work like that. How did the other guys take it?
Me: We were all kinda freaked out. And confused. It's like when you think you know someone, and all of a sudden, you find out there's this whole other side.
Jesus: Yeah. I feel the same way.
Me: What do you mean?

Jesus let out a big sigh. "Sometimes I feel like I'm two people. But it's more than just two sides of the same coin. It's like I'm Jesus... and I'm this other... thing. And sometimes I'm not sure which is which. "
He looked up at me hopefully, like maybe, just *maybe* I'd get it. Honestly, I didn't really, but he looked so hopeful, I tried to play along. "Yeah," I said.

We just sat for a while, neither of us knowing what else to say. Even though he was opening up to me, I still felt like I had no idea who this guy was. And it didn't help to find out he didn't seem to know who he was either. Maybe he was just crazy.
Jesus said, "you must think I'm crazy, huh?"
Crap! I hate it when he does that.
"No," I lied, "I think we all kinda feel like that sometimes."
"C'mon, Joel," he said, "out with it."

I took a deep breath. "Yeah, it does sound crazy. But no crazier than usual for you."

Jesus started laughing, and kept going, and then it was like he was crying a little, too.

"Thanks, Joel. I knew I could count on you."

"Huh!" I thought to myself. Desperate for an escape, and feeling a bit hungry, I said, "wanna go see if Ezra is cooking anything good?"

"Sure," Jesus said. "I could use some normality."

"Hey, maybe you could carve him another wooden bird on the way over."

"Wow. Jealous much?" he countered.

"Of you? Sheah, right."

We ran into Saul on the way. He gave Jesus a big hug and said, "thank God you're not invisible!" Jesus looked at me for an explanation, but I just shook my head, like, let it go.

Turned out Ezra *was* cooking, and he invited us in and put us to work, chopping and kneading and stuff. I think he was happy to have the company.

I can't say I'm glad Jesus chose to confide in me, but if he is someone special, like a prophet or something, then maybe it'll be like a bonus when I die. We'll see.

2:2

So I'm helping Eli chop wood again, and Jesus comes by.

"Hey, can I help?" he says.

Eli gives me a look, then hands Jesus an axe. "You know how to use one of these?"

Jesus says, "Hello - I'm a carpenter."

"This ain't about whittling birds, junior." Eli has been kind of snooty with Jesus ever since he disappeared and won't talk about what happened.

"Got it," Jesus says, and goes to work.

After a little while, Jesus says, "girls. Go figure, right?"

I get another look from Eli.

"Yeah, sure. You talking about anyone in particular?"

"Umm, maybe."

Now I happened to know that Jesus kinda likes Dara. I saw him write her name in the ground one day. He didn't hear me come up, but once he saw my shadow on her name, he dragged the stick across it.

"Well, from my vast experience," Eli starts in, "girls like it when you pay too much attention to them. And tease them. They always act all put out by it, but I know for a fact that they go tell their friends about it later."

"What do you tease them about?" Jesus asks.

Oh, no. Jesus is looking for advice on girls from Eli? What the hell is he thinking?

"Anything," says Eli. "Their clothes, what they say, how hot I am. Ya know. That sort of thing."

I wanted to say something because Jesus seemed to be taking this all in, and I was starting to feel sorry for him. I mean, it's not like I had any inside info, but Eli? Oye vey.

"So Eli, who do you have your sights set on these days?" I said, trying to get him off track.

"I don't know. Rachel is looking pretty good lately." Again with the Rachel thing. He just won't give up.

"I thought you finally gave up on her," I said.

"Well, some girls like to play hard to get," Eli answered. "And she knows that's the one way to get to me – acting like she couldn't care less."

"Like when she dumped that bucket of water on your head?" I asked.

"Foreplay, my friend. Foreplay."

"How do you figure?" asked Jesus.

"She wanted to see my wet robe all pressed up against my tight body."

"So how do I get Dara to notice me?" Jesus asks.

NO, JESUS, NO!!! I screamed in my head. But it was too late.

"Dara? Dara? Dude, don't waste your time. She's got some kind of attitude or aversion to the masculine gender. I tried getting her for like, *days*. She is one tough nut that ain't gonna crack with a novice like you."

"Oh, c'mon, Eli," I said, "maybe you're just not her type."

"She's *my* type, and that's what counts."

There was no way Jesus was buying all this. So why did he even ask? Could he really be so clueless when it comes to girls?

"I was going to carve her something," Jesus said. "Like a flower or something."

"Nah, don't waste your time till you get some kind of sign that she's interested."

I'm thinking – and when did that ever stop you, Eli? He probably just didn't want Jesus showing him up. I would have laid into Eli for his crappy advice, but I didn't want to make him look too bad. Usually if the other guys were around, we could all give him grief in a joking way. But Eli was already getting kinda high on himself lately, so I thought better of it. I mean, he's still my friend. And he was holding an axe.

We finally got all the chopping done, and I told Jesus I'd walk him to the well on the way home. As soon as we were out of earshot, I carefully scoped out the situation.

"Jesus, what the hell were you thinking, asking Eli for advice on girls?"

"What? He knows more than anyone else," Jesus said.

"He talks more about it than anyone else, but that doesn't mean he knows jack. When was the last time you saw him with a steady girl?"

Jesus didn't say anything.

"Exactly," I said.

"So what do I do?"

"Wait – doesn't being spiritually enlightened give you some sort of special insight on this?"

"Not as far as I can tell," Jesus said sort of disgustedly. "It's oddly not all that helpful with ordinary things."

"So you *are* interested in girls?"

"Well, yeaahh! What did you think?"

"I don't know, I don't know what the rules are! I don't really know anyone else who can heal stuff or fly to Joppa or read minds. I mean, you do get woodies and stuff, right?"

"Yes, if you must know, " Jesus said, all embarrassed. "I get them all the time."

"*All* the time?"

"Not *all* the time! C'mon!"

"So you have one now?"

Jesus laughed and gave me kind of a shove. "No!"

"Did you have one in Joppa?"

"Joel?"

"Yeah?"

"In the immortal words of Eli, shut the hell up."

"Uhhh, you swore! I bet all your powers are gone now."

"Don't say that!" he laughed. "Besides, it doesn't count if you're quoting."

I had to ask: "so what would you do if your powers were gone? Would you like, miss them?"

Jesus looked up at the sky for a while, then down at the ground. I thought to myself, if he starts drawing in the dirt, I'm outta here.

He looked at me and shrugged.

"Wow," I said, "that Joppa thing really got you rattled."

He just stood there quietly for a moment. "Yes."
 "No worries," I said. "I feel like I'm just getting to know you, even though I've known you for like, years."
Jesus smiled.
"You smile different, too," I said.
"Yeah?"
"Yeah, that creepy part is gone now."
Jesus shook his head. "Joel, for better or worse, I can always count on you for the truth."
"What is truth?" I asked, just to put it out there.
"Ha! Now there's a good question."
"So, Dara, huh?"
"Yeah?"
"What's your plan?
He shrugged again.
I told him, "the carved flower sounds pretty cool."
"You think? Seriously?"
"Yeah. Totally."
We both smiled.
"Well, I should get home," I said. "later, nutjob."
After I was several yards away, I heard him say quietly, "Later, friend."

2:3

Saturday night, and I figured it would be the same old, same old, but boy was I wrong. We were all there except for Ezra – can't remember why.
Saul says, "hey Jesus, how about turning some more water into wine. It was you that one time, wasn't it?"

Jesus sighs and says, "you don't understand and I don't want to talk about it."

"Man," says Eli, "you are such a downer lately."

Owen says, "hey, lay off. The guy's had it tough lately."

"A minor set-back," I add.

"Hmm," says Jesus.

Eli says, "what you need is to get laid."

"Eli!" says Tobiah, "not everything is resolved by sex, or even by thinking about sex."

"Phht, how would you know, virgin," Eli says under his breath.

"You are such a jerk," says Tobiah.

"Guys, please don't argue on my account." Jesus says.

Saul continues, "so, not even like a cup?"

We all say, "Saauuuul!"

"Alright, alright! So you've given up?"

"No, I haven't given up," Jesus sighs. "It's like, I've spent my whole life feeling pretty cool about where I was headed, and then all of a sudden, boom, I feel like I have no control over anything in my life."

Oren speaks up. "I don't know, Jesus, that kind of happens to me on a daily basis. Well, okay, weekly."

I ask, "for instance?"

"For instance, I've been dating this girl and…"

"Whoa to the whoa!" says Eli. "You've been dating?"

"Yes, if you must know, Leah and I have been seeing each other."

"For how long," says Eli, "an hour?"

"No," says Oren calmly, "about three months."

"Oh," says Saul, "so that's where you've been."

"As I was saying…"

Eli jumps in: "So what's she like? I mean, you know, does she…"

"AS I WAS SAYING, just when you feel like you understand the relationship, and things are cool, she suddenly gets upset about something you didn't do, even though you've never done it before and didn't even know she wanted it done."

"Like bone her?" Eli snorts.

We all had to jump up at that point and stop Oren from punching Eli. And believe me, it took all of us.

Tobiah finally says something. "Eli, what is your problem? You've been pissed off for about a week, and I'm tired of it. If something's wrong, tell us, but stop being such an ass!"

"Oh," Eli says back, "and who made *you* the leader?"

"He's only saying what we all think," I said.

Eli got this very hurt look on his face. Not just the 'I'm looking hurt on purpose so you guys will lay off me' look, it was a real down to the toes hurt look.

"Oh, yeah?" he says.

Oren and Saul say, "yeah!"

"It's kind of like when Joel wouldn't forgive Jesus," Saul adds.

"Thanks, buddy," I said to Saul.

Saul says in all sincerity, "no problem, pal!"

Jesus says, "look, Eli, *some*thing must be bothering you. Talk to us."

Eli just stood and looked at us for a while, and then, and I would NOT have believed it if I hadn't seen it with my own eyes, he started to tear up. I have *never* seen Eli get choked up.

"You can all go to hell," he says in shaky voice, and walks off.

We all called his name and told him to come back, but he just kept walking. Tobiah quoted, (I mean, I'm assuming it was a quote), "pride goeth before destruction, and an haughty spirit before a fall." Jesus added, "the world and the pride of the world passes away; but anyone who does God's will endures."

Tobiah got this troubled look on his face. "Where in the Torah is that from?"

"Just made it up," says Jesus.

"Right." says Tobiah.

Finally, after a few days I went over to see Eli. We had all decided to leave him alone and either let him tell us what was bugging him or just get over himself. But that wasn't working. Just as I knocked on Eli's door, the door opened and Ezra was standing there. It must have been like a mirror, cause he looked just as surprised as I was.

"Oh, Joel! Hi. What are you doing here?"

I checked the house to make sure I was at Eli's and said, "Ezra! Is Eli here?"

"Eli? Oh, Eli! Yes, of course. It's his house, after all, right?" Ezra sputtered out.

"Riiiight'" I said as he stepped back and I walked in.

"Eli!" Ezra called out.

"Yeah, babe?" I heard Eli say from his room.

"Joel is here!" Ezra said, just as Eli walked in, wearing just his skivvies.

Eli froze. I froze. Ezra just stood there smiling and sweating.

Maybe it was a few seconds, but I swear it felt like I passed at least one more birthday standing there.

"Shit," said Eli.

"Umm," I said, "guess I came at a bad time. Pardon the expression."

Ezra said, "no, no, it wasn't like that!"

Eli said, "Joel, I'm not, we're not…"

I asked, "and you called Ezra 'babe' because…?"

Another birthday passed.

"Sit down," Eli said.

He started to, too, but I said, "dude, put some clothes on first, huh?"

He came back with his robe on, and sat down next to Ezra. "We're… friends."

"Friends?" I repeated.

"Well…" Ezra started.

"*Friends!*" Eli said loudly. "He's helping me with my clothes, okay?"

"Why?"

"Cause I need to do *something*! I can't get any girls to even *talk* to me!"

I asked, "so you're…"

"I'm fucking lonely, okay?" said Eli.

"So, you guys aren't, like…"

"No!" said Ezra.

"Hell, no!" said Eli.

"Now Eli," Ezra says, "no need to be mean. Remember?"

"Right. Okay. Sorry."

I was amazed! Ezra got Eli to apologize for being Eli! I didn't know what was going on between them, but that alone was pretty damn shocking!

"So why did you call him 'babe,' and why didn't you have your clothes on?" I asked.

"He was on his way out and I had *just* taken off the new robe he picked out for me. Look, come see it."

We walked into his room, and there on the bed was a really cool, blue robe, brand new, nice soft material, obviously not cheap. "wow," I said, "that really is nice."

"Thank you," said Ezra, super proud of himself.

"And 'babe'?" I asked.

Ezra said, "That's his nickname for me, because he says I'm more like a girl: a 'babe'. Yeah, it's kinda demeaning, but hey, it's a nickname, they're not supposed to be flattering. And it's the first one I've ever had. Okay?"

"See?" Eli said. "*Friends!*"

"Okay," I said.

Eli grabbed me by the shoulders, "but you cannot, *cannot*, tell the guys!"

"Okay, okay! But, Eli, we're your friends, too. You can talk to us."

Eli stood up straighter and said, "I'm a proud man, Joel. Maybe too proud, but there you have it. Ezra is helping me with that, too."
"All true," said Ezra.

So there you have it. Who would have thought it? Do I believe their story? Well…

2:4

Oren was freaking out. Normally calm as a cucumber, it takes a hell of a lot to get him riled up. But at that moment, even his sweat was sweating.

"I can't do it!" he said in a deep voice. "What if I mess it up? My life will be ruined!"
He'd been going on like this the whole way over to Leah's house. We had gotten so close, then he started marching back the way we'd come. We managed to stop him somewhere in the middle of the market.

Ezra said, "you're being a bit overdramatic, don't you think?"
"You don't understand," he said, "I love her!"
"Then go talk to her dad!" Ezra countered.
"But what if he says no?" Oren said, with big fish eyes.
"Oh, well, then yeah, you'd be screwed," Ezra said.
Oren let out a groan that got everyone looking at us standing in the middle of the market.

"I'm kidding!" Ezra said. "Just go ask and stop torturing yourself!"

Oren had been seeing Leah on the sly, and now he was sure (well, pretty sure) that she was the one for him. All he had to do was go talk to her dad, and then he'd be set to marry her. He knew she really liked him, and she was unattached. The guy her folks had fixed her up with had recently died a rather tragic death. Leah had never actually met him, but he didn't sound like the brightest guy.

While traveling in a far country, (his family was in the import/export business) the guy went into a bar and overheard two other guys talking about a buried treasure. The two guys wound up arguing and eventually going into the street and killing each other. Leah's guy picks up the treasure map, and actually finds the treasure. It's like this *huge* chest of gold coins, just like you'd think. Well, he got it all loaded up, was feeling like life was pretty damn good, and noticed a single coin on the ground, right behind his donkey. He bent down to pick it up and the donkey kicked him in the head and he died. At least that's the story I heard.

So now the field was clear for Oren.
"Dude, it's like God has cleared the way for you," I told him. 'Right, Jesus?"
"Umm," Jesus mumbled, "I don't think it really works that way."
I asked, "why else would God kill the other guy?"
"God doesn't kill people," Jesus said.

Tobiah perked up. "So why do people die?"
Jesus said, "actually they don't. Not really."

Oren said, "guys! Focus! A little help, huh?"
"Hang on, Oren, Leah's not going anywhere," Tobiah
said. "If people don't die, then what happens to
them?"
"You guys are making my head hurt," Eli yelled.
"Oren, grow some balls and go talk to the dad, or
else you don't even deserve her. Jesus, stop talking
nonsense before I smack you upside the head.
Tobiah, who the hell cares about death? We're
young! Save that for when you're like, thirty."

There was a stunned silence. Oren kind of shook his
head, and said, "wow, you're right." And with that,
he started walking toward Leah's house with new
resolve.
"See!" Eli continues, "I *am* right sometimes. Enough
with the sappy stuff."
Ezra gave Eli a big smile, and they wandered over to
the market stalls.

Tobiah was like a dog on a hunt. "Jesus, answer my
question."
Jesus said, "yes, of course, we all leave this earth, but
there's more."
"More what?" Tobiah asked.
"More life," Jesus answered.
"And to what passages in the Torah do you equate
this *belief*?" asked Tobiah.
"I don't know that it does equate. It's just something
I know," Jesus said.

"Jesus, you drive me crazy! First, you do this crazy healing and disappearing stuff and then you won't talk about it, and then you postulate about the afterlife based on nothing more than a feeling! How do you expect to be any kind of a prophet, much less a religious scholar, if you can't even give some sort of logical, reasoned answer? People are going to string you up for being such an irresponsible theologian, or worse, they'll simply ignore you! If you're going to go around saying there's no such thing as death, when there *is* death, like... right over there in that *butcher's* shop, then you'd damn well better provide some sort of argument that's pretty conclusive! Jesus! Are you even listening?"

"I will provide an argument," Jesus said softly.

"Okay, let's see it!" Tobiah said.

"Some day," Jesus answered.

"Some day? *Some day*? Well, I hope you're gearing up for it, because it's gonna have to be a pretty good trick!"

I finally got into it. "Tobiah, that's a pretty tough thing to prove. I mean, think about what you're asking for. What's he going to do, bring someone back to life after they die?"

"Of course not, don't be ridiculous," Tobiah scoffed.

Saul suddenly spoke up. "Tobiah, what's your proof that he's wrong?"

Tobiah looked baffled. "What's my proof? Things die! *People* die!"

Saul said, "yeah, but remember what Jesus said about God being like a shepherd? What shepherd wants to have his sheep killed? He needs the wool, right? Well, I guess they do eat them sometimes. I don't know, I just felt so good when Jesus said all that stuff that one night. Even you liked it."

Tobiah stood there, started to say something, then just stood there with his finger pointing at us. Then he walked away grumbling to himself.

Saul put his hand on Jesus' shoulder. "Don't worry about Tobiah. He gets a little too into his head sometimes."
Jesus kind of blinked a little. "Saul?"
"Yeah?"
"You are like a… "
"Yeah? A what..?" Saul asked, not exactly sure what to expect.
"I don't know, like a big thing that's hard to move. An elephant? No, that's not right. They move."
"A wall?" I suggested.
"A door!" Saul said. "But one that's closed? And like, locked?"
Jesus said, "nah. I don't know. But hey, thanks anyway."
"So it's like a good thing, right?" Saul asked.
"OH yeah!" Jesus said.

From a few streets over, even over the noise of the market, we heard Oren's voice.
"Whahooooooooooooooooooooooooooooooooooooooooo oooooo!"
"Boys," Saul said, "it's time to celebrate."

2:5

Getting married – biggest thing in your life, right? So you want to party like it's the end of the world – right? Well how the hell do you do that in a dinky little town like Nazareth? We kept trying to come up with something cool and exciting and cheap, but we couldn't think of a damn thing.

Another trip to prostitute street?
"No way," said Oren. "I'm not going to give anyone an excuse for me not to marry Leah."

Another drunken donkey night?
"No way," Jesus said. "I'm not comfortable doing the wine thing again."
"Why not?" asked a very disappointed Saul.
"What if it turns out wrong. Like Joppa? I could poison everybody."
"Oh. Yeah," Saul said with bug eyes.

A quick trip to Joppa?
"STOP ASKING!" Jesus said.
"Easy there, guy," I told him. I'd never heard him raise his voice before.
He was still kinda pissed, but in like a fussy way.
"What's wrong with walking? Walking is a perfectly acceptable form of transportation. I've walked it. Have you walked it? I don't think so. You should try it. It's invigorating."

The last comment made me phhht – that noise when your lips are closed but you have to laugh anyway – because I could still picture how miserable he looked that night when he walked the whole thing by himself. Jesus punched me.

"Ow," I said.

Suddenly Oren said, "yeah, *let's* walk to Joppa! We could camp out along the way and hang out at the beach. Come on! It'll be an adventure!"

"Too far," said Eli with authority.

Tobiah said, "how about Caesarea? Big town, by the sea, about half as far?"

"Yeah, okay," Eli said, never one to show much enthusiasm.

"This will be awesome!" Saul yelled.

"I hear they have theatres there," Ezra put in.

"And sports!" Saul added.

"Road trip!" we all started yelling.

 The next thing was to get permission and some traveling money from our parents. My dad was pretty skeptical about it at first, but once I appealed to the sentimental memories of his own youth, he totally got it and said okay. He even gave me a few extra shekels. It meant a lot to me. This was clearly a once in a lifetime thing.

It was a beautiful morning and it was a great feeling – being with your friends and being free and on your way to something fun. It was also a little scary cause none of us (other than Jesus) had ever been beyond Galilee. And now we were headed for a big city on the coast of Samaria! Fuckin' A!

Ezra showed up with a ton of food so we wouldn't have to spend too much on that. Or so we thought. Eli was late, of course. Saul was so excited I thought he was going to run the whole way. We talked a lot about what we were going to do once we got there. We had a whole day but only a day, so depending on how we looked at it, it filled and flattened like a water bag. Ezra, Jesus and Tobiah wanted to catch a show at the amphitheatre, but wondered if they could follow something in Latin. Caesarea is a Roman port town, so a lot of it was geared for them. The rest of us were hoping there would be some sports going on – gladiators and stuff. But we all wanted to spend the day seeing the sights, checking out the beach, and hopefully the girls!

About two hours into the walk, we passed some Roman soldiers marching in formation. Gulp! I made sure I was looking the other way, not that they knew who had nailed one of them with an egg awhile back. I still got nervous. Maybe it wasn't even the same guys.

About lunch time we found a spot under some trees to have lunch and completely devoured every crumb of food Ezra had brought. He was a little bummed that we didn't leave any for later, but we made up for it with lots of compliments, both verbal and gaseous.

Fortunately it wasn't too hot out, but by the time the sun set, we were all pretty beat. We were only at Narbata, which was still a good hour or two outside of Caesarea, but decided to call it a day. It's a little town like Nazareth, and we felt okay about knocking on the door of a butcher shop to get some food. The guy was pretty nice, but just sold us a few chickens and said goodnight. We found a spot on the outskirts and built a fire and cooked the birds, rubbing them first with some wild herbs Ezra found. We were so hungry it tasted like the best meal we'd ever had. Unfortunately, it went pretty fast and we all could have eaten a lot more. The wind was kicking up, and since we couldn't afford an inn, Jesus suggested we hunker down in a stable we passed earlier. It was a really good idea, except for the smell. We kept telling Oren it was him.

When the morning came, we woke up to Saul trying to milk a cow. He made a real ruckus, that bull, as you can probably imagine. Tobiah grabbed Saul and pointed him towards the female cow and then collapsed back onto his hay pile. In a little while, the stable owner came out and took the full bucket of milk from Saul, and went back into the house without saying a word. Guess that was our payment for having a roof over our heads.

We headed off hungry and as we got nearer to Caesarea found a number of make-shift stalls where we could buy bread and dates and stuff. As we got even closer, it was like there was music playing, loud happy music that got louder and louder as we got farther and farther
into the city. We could feel the breeze and smell the salt air, and what with all the people and noises and

colors, it was like being at a festival. And it was just an ordinary day!

So we walked around the market and saw all sorts of cool stuff that nobody bothers to haul all the way out to Nazareth. Some of it must have come from Rome and Spain. We all found things we liked, but didn't want to spend our money too soon. We saw some crazy animals for sale, too. Huge scary birds, a bunch of different kinds of monkeys and even a lion!

"See, Oren" Eli said, "*that*'s what a lion looks like. Please observe the smallness of his butt." Which started that whole debate again.

We saw some Roman girls walking around, but they wore this crazy make-up on their eyes that made them look like freaks. And they looked at us like we were a bunch of hicks. Which we are. But still.

It was starting to get hot, so we went to check out this huge tower King Herod built overlooking the water. We climbed around the rocks and looked out at the water and all the boats going in and out of the harbor. The water was so beautiful; it wasn't like anything I'd ever seen before. We started walking along the edge of the water, and we came up to these fishermen.

"How's business?" Eli says.
"Too many fish, not enough hands." says the fisherman. "Say, you boys want to help bring in the next load?"

We all sort of stood there, not sure what to say. "Tell you what," the guy went on, "since I'm really short-handed today, if you go out and help for say, an hour or two, you can come back at dinner and have all the fish you can eat. And if you come back before dinner, I'll take out on the boat just to see the sunset. What do you say?"

We all kind of looked at each other. I was pretty psyched about being out on the water, so I spoke up. "Sure!" Turns out the other guys were okay with it, too. Well, Tobiah doesn't really like water, but I think he went along quietly because he didn't want to look bad.

And before you know it, there we were, a bunch of Nazarene goofballs hauling nets out on the great blue sea off Caesarea! It was awesome! Even that fishy smell when we pulled them in was kind of exotic or something, and made me think I should just stay and live out there forever. The couple of hours turned into three, but actually went pretty fast, and too soon for me we were back on shore. Ezra didn't much like the fish flopping around in the boat and Tobiah was looking a bit green; Saul was kinda fumbly, but did okay and Oren moved really slowly because he thought this whole being out on the water thing was pretty sketchy. But Jesus and I felt great. We saw each other beaming and beamed back at each other.

Once we were back on dry land, I asked him, "Jesus, was that awesome, or what?"
"Oh, man! I love being on the sea!" he said.
"I'm ready to live here!"

"Totally! I might have to start popping out here instead of Joppa!" Jesus said.

"Really?!!"

"No, dude," he laughed. But then he said, "I don't know. Maybe someday I'll come back. This *is* pretty great."

Tobiah had kind of walked away down the beach, and Saul said, "hey, Tobes, you okay?"

Tobiah turned back and said, "I think I'm gonna hurl."

Jesus walked right over and put his hand on Tobiah's head. They just stood there a second. And then Tobiah looked up.

"Whoa," he said. "I feel better."

"Good," Jesus said.

"I feel a lot better. Thank you."

"No problem."

"How do you do that?"

At that point, we were all standing around them.

Jesus looked down. "Tobiah, please. I will tell you in my own time. I'm really not trying to make you mad. I just want to enjoy the day. It's been a really good day for me. Please."

Just then Samuel, the fisherman came up. "Thank you, boys! Come back in a couple of hours. Don't forget!"

2:6

Since we had a couple of hours to kill before our return to the beach for dinner, we went back into Caesarea to scope out the local entertainment. No plays going on, and the gladiators weren't performing till the next day. Dang. But we figured maybe they were practicing, so we went to check it out. We went by the stadium and could actually hear swords clanging, and every once in a while a loud groan, which was pretty cool. Oren and Eli wanted to wait and see if any of the gladiators came out, so the rest of us went over to the amphitheatre.

It was huge! And this guy who was doing some masonry work to the steps told us that because of the way it was built you could hear everything from even the back row. So we ran around and tried it, and went up to the stage and sang and whispered and yelled, and we had a pretty good time. The stonemason just kept laughing at us.

When we walked back over towards the stadium, Oren and Eli were coming down the street practically skipping. They'd met one of the gladiators as he was coming out, Marius, this gladiator that we'd even heard of in Nazareth. They said he was massively huge and really cool and invited all of us to a party that night. We thought maybe they were joking, but they swore they weren't. It sounded too good to be true.

We headed back down to the beach, and there was our guy, Samuel, waving us to wade out and get in his boat. We all got in, even Tobiah, and it was the best part of the trip for me. The wind was up and the light was kind of orangey and the water was blue as… well, I don't know what. I've never felt so alive. It was definitely more fun for everybody because we weren't trying to haul nets or avoid the sail or follow Samuel's orders. We could just sit back and enjoy it. Samuel even let me steer for a while. I was in heaven.

Back on shore, Samuel's family had already built a fire and they were just slapping the fish down to cook. Apparently, he has just one son but a bunch of daughters. His son, who we met earlier, was pretty cool, and the daughters were a riot. They were really tough and funny and were making cracks about their dad the whole time, but just this side of disrespectful, so he was laughing along with them. And one of the daughters was pretty good looking. I think she was a little younger than me, and her name was Nissa. She sat next to me, so we got to talk awhile. It was cool. And his wife just kept giving us more fish and bread till we thought we would burst. Over all, it was a great meal, and I had a great time hanging out by the firelight, with the waves quietly rumbling like music.

After a while, Samuel and his family packed up and went home cause they had be up early to fish again the next day. I was kind of jealous. Nissa even looked back and gave me a little wave. I pulled Jesus aside and asked him, "hey, what do you think would happen if we came back tomorrow and helped again?"

"Joel," Jesus said, "you're reading my mind."

"Should we?"

"Actually," Jesus said, "my parents will freak out if I don't get back on time."

"Even just a day?"

"Yeah," he went on, "I did that once when I was younger and they're kind of paranoid about it now. And then the whole Joppa thing. They like to keep a close watch."

I was kinda bummed. I would have loved to stay, but not by myself. It had been like the perfect day and evening, and I couldn't imagine a better life. Maybe I'd come back some day.

Since it was now dark, Eli and Oren were ready to head over to the gladiators' party, so we followed them, wondering if this was for real. We got to this big house with all these Romans going in. It looked like a pretty swanky deal. Romans aren't as modest as us, so there was quite a bit of skin showing, especially the ladies. Some of them, even the guys, really had the make-up caked on. But typical of Eli, he went right up and walked in with a bunch of other people. The gladiator, Marius, was standing just inside the door greeting people, and he shook Eli's hand. Eli motioned for us to come in, and Marius directed us to this back room. He was wearing this robe that was practically see-through, and he wasn't wearing anything underneath. That should have been our first tip-off.

We made our way through his house, which was kind of smoky from all the torches, and I almost stepped in this stupid fountain in the middle of the floor (who puts a fountain in the middle of the floor in a house?). He ushered us through a curtain and left us. Inside there were a bunch of people working and getting into costumes and stuff. This weird old guy was in charge and he acted like he'd been waiting for us. "Quick, get into your costumes and make-up and get out there with the food!" We'd been had. Marius wasn't being friendly, he was getting us for cheap labor. Or maybe he really was trying to do us a favor, but we could see we weren't in any position to ask him about it. We all kind of looked at each other, like, so now what? Ezra shrugged and went over to get his costume. It was kind of flimsy and bright orange and then they painted his lips and cheeks, and stuck an orange wig on his head and handed him a tray of stuff. He waved and went out. Tobiah was shaking his head, and Oren and Jesus were looking for a way out. Eli looked pretty sad and confused, and Saul and I were weighing it over in our heads. At least I think that's what was going on with Saul – it's hard to tell sometimes.

As the other guys were making their way out the back, I said, "Saul, what do you think?"
"I wonder if we get to eat the food we're serving," he said.
"Do you want to stay and see how crazy it gets, or do you want to scram?"
Just about then, Ezra came back with his tray empty already. His eyes were about as big as the tray.

"I just got groped five times. Twice by Marius."
Saul said, "let's get out of here."

Ezra grabbed his clothes and we went out the back,
the weird old guy yelling at us. Out in the alley, the
other guys were just hanging out waiting for us. Eli
looked like he was going to cry. I guess he'd felt
pretty good about getting in good with a celebrity,
and now he was standing in the back alley where it
smelled like week-old crap. Off in the distance, we
heard the rumble of thunder.

We wandered back down to the harbor and sat
throwing rocks into the water. It sucked. We'd had
this great trip, a fantastic evening, and then
humiliation at the massive hands of the only celebrity
we'd probably ever meet.

Eli said, "Oren, wipe that goddamn smile off your
face."
Ezra jumped right in. "Eli. Remember what we
talked about? Just cause you're mad, you don't have
to lash out at others."
Eli let out a big sigh. "Yeah. Sorry, Oren. But do you
have to smile *all* the time?"
Oren said, "I just remembered that I'm marrying the
most wonderful girl in the world. How can I not
smile?"
Saul starts laughing and pointing at Eli. "Dude, you
just got schooled! By Ezra!"
"And what's that supposed to mean?" Ezra said in
his cold voice. He doesn't use it often, but it's
definitely chilly.
"Nothing," Saul backed down.

"Guys," Oren said, "be nice to each other!"

"Fucking Marius," Eli said.

"I imagine someone probably is about now," Tobiah said. "I wish the all the Romans would leave and never come back."

Oren said, "come on, this has been a good trip. We've had some adventure! And we saw lots of stuff we've never seen before."

"Yeah," Saul said, "it has been pretty cool."

"Best part?" I asked, having already picked out mine.

Ezra said, "running around the amphitheatre."

Saul said, "dinner by the sea."

Jesus said, "being out on the sea."

I said, "yeah, same here."

Tobiah said, "hearing Saul try to milk a bull."

Saul said, "shut up, Tobiah."

Eli said, "seeing Ezra in that stupid get-up." He gave Ezra a smile.

Oren said, "being with you guys."

"Group hug!" Ezra called out. No one moved. "Okay, *fine*."

We all just stood and looked out at the water, and then slowly headed back to Nazareth as it started to rain.

2:7

It was around midnight when we started walking back to Nazareth from our road trip to Caesarea. We heard thunder, but the storm must have stayed at sea, cause it was just rumblings and rain for us. We were totally beat, but we kept going till we came to the stable outside of Narbata where we'd stopped on the way out. We were soaked and tired and we didn't really care about the smell this time. And we didn't blame Oren for it – we all fell asleep within seconds.

When I finally woke up and remembered where I was, I felt weird about going home. Good and sad, both. I could still smell the sea and imagine the water glistening in the sun, and I swear I got a little stiff thinking about it. Or maybe that was cause I also thought of Nissa and her little wave as she left. Would life ever be as good as that night on the beach? If I ever decide to go back, will it still be there? Or will it be too late?

I definitely want to go back some day. But I would feel bad leaving my dad. My mom died when I was just a little kid, and my leaving would be hard on him. I still kind of miss her. It's hard to remember her exactly, but I sometimes miss the feeling of her, ya know? Maybe that's what Jesus was trying to say to Tobiah about death, that day in the market. That if I can still feel her, she's still around somewhere. Not like a ghost, though. Like a presence or something.

Once the others woke up, we realized that most of the animals had been taken outside, but someone had left a jug of milk and some sweet cakes on top of a barrel for us. We'd slept through all of it. Saul was the last to wake up, so Ezra put the orange wig on his sleeping head and we all got a kick out of that. When Saul did wake up, he decided to wear it anyway. He's a good sport that way.

We finally met our hosts as we were heading off. The mister was kinda grouchy, but the misses was really nice and kinda shy. Their four sons were all off and married, so she really liked having us in their stable. We thanked her a lot. For me it was kinda like that mom feeling I was just talking about. Saul gave her the orange wig, and she laughed and laughed about it, but was too embarrassed to put it on.

So hours later we're walking along and Saul says, "Oren, how do you know Leah is the *one*?
There was a long pause as we trudged along.
"Umm," Oren said, "What do you mean?"
"What if you find someone that you like better next week?"
"Oh, Saul," Tobiah said.
"No, I'm just asking!" Saul said.
Another long pause.

Oren finally said, "she makes my day. I think of her when I first wake up and when I fall asleep. And I want to be with her as much as I can. And she's funny and cute. And if I wait to see if there's someone better, then I might lose her."

Ezra said, "wow. I hope someone feels that way about me sometime."

"So," Saul continued, "there wasn't like a sign or something?"

"What kind of sign?" Oren asked.

"I don't know. Like a voice or a ringing or the earth shaking or a bird landing on her?"

"No," laughed Oren. "I just feel it."

"Like God's love," said Jesus under his breath.

"What was that?" Tobiah asked.

"What? Did I say something?" Jesus said.

"You said, 'like God's love,'" Saul said.

Jesus winced. I was half expecting him to disappear again, even at the risk of winding up in a tree in Joppa.

"What does love have to do with anything?" Tobiah asked kind of loudly. "It's just a bunch of sap. Eli, back me up here."

Eli said, "sorry, man. I know you guys will laugh, but I'm learning that being cool is better than being selfish. You just feel better about yourself."

Ezra said, "see? I'm right. It is the secret ingredient."

Jesus said, "Tobiah, why is this so important to you?

Tobiah said, "what do you mean?"

"Why are you always getting so upset about this?"

"You just… okay, the reason is… if you're going to…" sputtered Tobiah.

Saul was trying not to laugh too hard. Tobiah shot him a look and then yelled at Jesus, "you're not taking this prophet thing seriously!"

Jesus just looked at him. "So you think I *am* a prophet?"

"I think you *could* be! But Jesus, you can't half-ass it! Nobody likes a lame prophet. It's a contradiction in terms!"

"Okay," Jesus said. "I'll try harder. But I really, really appreciate your concern. I didn't realize it meant so much to you."

"It doesn't," Tobiah said. "Not much, anyway. It's just if you're going to do it, do it *right*."

Jesus finally said, "Tobiah, how did you feel yesterday when you didn't hurl?"

Tobiah blinked a few times but didn't answer.

"Loved?" Ezra suggested.

"Ha!" Eli laughed. "He got you there!"

"Shut up, Eli," Tobiah said, "I'm still thinking."

"And how does it feel when your family embraces you?" asked Jesus.

Tobiah blinked some more, but this time his eyes were watery.

"Okay, now imagine an endless supply of that," Jesus said. "That's God."

Tobiah stepped off the road and leaned against a tree, his shoulders shaking. Saul left him alone for a minute, then went over and put his arm around his twin brother's shoulder. We tried not to watch.

Saul told me later what they said. He swore me to secrecy, so don't tell anyone.

Tobiah: It's not fair.
Saul: What?

Tobiah: I study and study and study and I never get any closer. And then Jesus comes along and blows it all away with his tricks and his love-talk, and he doesn't even try. And he's not even that good at it! Saul: I know. It totally sucks.
Tobiah: Even you.
Saul: What?
Tobiah: It's like you get it, and you don't try either.
Saul: Yeah. I suck, too.
Tobiah: Saul, you don't have to agree with everything I say.
Saul: You're right, I don't.
Tobiah: You're a moron.
Saul: You are, too.
Tobiah. I know. I know. (*starts crying again*)
Saul: What now?
Tobiah: Nothing. It's just that sometimes… I wish I was more like you.

Saul leaned his head down to touch his brother's head. "See, you are a moron."
Tobiah took a deep breath, rubbed his eyes and wiped the snot off his nose. "Okay, let's get going. We've got a long road ahead."

They joined up with us and we started walking again. Nobody said anything for quite a while.

It was well after dark by the time we got home. We'd had a good trip, and we all smacked Oren on the back since it was his engagement that started it all. When I got home my dad had dinner waiting for me.

"So, how was the trip?" he asked.

"Really good."

"Any trouble?" he asked.

"Surprisingly, no," I said, smiling.

"Any money left over?"

"A little," I told him.

"Good! Glad you're back," he said, and started shuffling off to bed.

"Hey, Dad?"

"Yes?"

"Some day... nevermind. I'll tell you later."

2:8

So one morning, Jesus stops by and asks if I want to go for a walk with him. I wasn't sure what to expect. I mean, I'd seen him walking around on his own, so why did he need me? Were we gonna *talk*? Like, the whole time? I was getting to where I honestly liked the guy, but it's not like I'm really the listening type. At least I don't see myself that way. Whatever.

We started walking up a trail into the hills. It was a hot day, and we were hoping for a breeze up there. No talking for awhile, and then all of a sudden, Jesus says, "so, do you dream about the sea?"

"Only when I'm awake," I tell him.

He laughed. "I'm going back there someday," he said.

"Yeah, me, too. Maybe we could work for Samuel for a few years and then get our own boat."

"That would be sweet," he agreed. "But I wouldn't plan on it."

"Why not?"

He let out a big sigh. "My life is pretty well planned out, I guess."

"You guess?"

"I don't know."

"You don't seem real psyched about this prophet stuff. In fact, it seems like you dread it."

He stopped and looked around, like he wanted to make sure no one was listening. He even looked up in the sky. I thought to myself, "oh boy, here we go."

"It's almost like the sea. I can hear it calling, but I'm not sure I want to answer. I mean, the sea, yeah, in a heartbeat. But what if this is set in stone? What if the prophet path is irreversible? What if it only *seems* like there's a choice and the choice has already been made?"

We looked down at the town.

"Is there anything you *like* about the prophet stuff?" I asked.

"I like healing people. That's pretty cool, except it usually freaks people out."

"Can you just do that part of it?"

"I'm guessing not," he answered. "Once I start doing that, people want to know how it works. Like Tobiah."

"Tobiah is just trying to help. I think."

"Yeah, I know. But it's almost like he's my third parent. It would be nice if I could figure this out on my own, without all the pressure."

"What if you're not really a prophet? What if you're just a guy who heals?"

"Then I'm screwed," Jesus said. "Because sooner or later, I'm going to have to start talking about this stuff, and if the talk doesn't come with the walk, then I'm still in trouble."

"That one night in the field you were great! What was wrong with that?"

"I don't know," Jesus said. "It's kind of like with Joppa. What if I can't do it every time? What if I *am* a prophet and I'm just not a very good one?"

We started walking again, and I honestly didn't know what to tell the guy. It wasn't like I had figured anything out in *my* life. Same old questions went through my mind about whether he was confused, nutty or just certifiable.

"You can always come fishing with me," I told him. And I was surprised to realize that I actually meant it. He kept walking but looked back and smiled at me. A real smile. Then he stopped walking so suddenly that I thought maybe he'd spotted a snake.

"Hey," he said, "maybe I could do both? Like, do my messiah thing - only at the beach?"

"Maybe you just need to practice your routine," I told him. "Why don't you use me as a test?"

"Now?" he asked.

"Sure, why not?"

"Umm, okay. Actually, I did have this idea the other day."

"Hit me."

"In the world of God…"

"Whoa, whoa, whoa. 'The world of God?' What are you talking about?"

"Well, like, being in touch with God."

"'In touch with God?' A little too touchy-feely. Maybe use something people can relate to."

"Country of God?"

"And not the city?"

"Kingdom of God?"

"Too political"

"Realm?"

"Let's come back to that."

"Okay. The blah blah blah is like when a man hides his wife in the attic and won't let her out."

"What the hell are you talking about?"

"You know, when you have something that's really great and rare and you don't want anyone to take it?"

"Yeeaaaah…"

"So you lock it away. To keep it safe."

"Seems kind of rough to keep a wife locked away in an attic."

"I thought it was a pretty good analogy."

"Maybe if it wasn't a wife. How about a dog? Or what if it was like a valuable *thing*."

"Yeah, yeah. Like what?"

"I don't know. A treasure?"

"No, I don't want people to think it's all about wealth."

"It's not?"

"No."

"Not even a little?"

"Nope."

"Damn."

"What?"

"I was just kind of hoping. I mean, having money is pretty cool. I was kind of hoping if I got more religious, I'd have more cash."

"No. Not at all."

"Crap! You're sure?"

"Completely. But getting back to the thing…"

"Man! God doesn't love money?"

"God doesn't know anything about money."

"Then why does it exist?"

"Joel, *focus*. If you could have one thing that you really valued, what would it be?"

"A boatload of cash."

"Okay, I think we're done." He started walking again.

"Are you mad at me?" I asked him.

"No, no," he said in his peeved voice. "I'll just keep thinking. I've got plenty of time."

"Okay."

We walked for a while in silence. "So how big a fishing boat would you want to get?" I asked him. We managed to talk about our joint fishing venture until we made it back into town, a good hour later.

2:9

Tobiah, Saul, Jesus and I were sitting outside the twin's house on a hot, boring afternoon. The twins' mom had chased us out cause we kept getting in her way while she cleaned.

Saul: What do you guys wanna do?

Tobiah: Nothing.

Saul: We could go see if Ezra is cooking.

Tobiah: Yeah, sure!

Me: Hey, Tobiah, don't you have class with the rabbi?

Tobiah: Nope. I gave all that up.

Jesus: What?

Tobiah: I gave it up.

Saul: (*to Jesus*) Ask him why.

Tobiah: Saul. Chill.

Saul: Ask him.

Me: Okay, why did you give it up?

Tobiah: I just don't get it anymore. It's a bunch of old stories that have no relation to today and I'm not getting any clearer about God and the way the world works, so why bother?

Jesus: Huh!

Tobiah: What?

Jesus: Nothing, just... huh!

Saul: So; Ezra's?

Jesus: (*to Tobiah*) Is it my fault?

Tobiah: No, no, no. Not really. Yeah, pretty much.

Jesus: See, *that*'s why I don't like to talk about it.

Tobiah: I'm not mad at you or anything. I actually feel much better now.

Jesus: But I thought you liked being all scholarly.

Tobiah: I did. Now I don't. Seriously, it's fine.

Jesus: Huh!

Saul: So; Ezra's?

Jesus: I can't help feeling responsible for this. Like I took something away from you.

Tobiah: You can't take something away that I never really had.

Me: Whoa – that was deep!

Jesus: So you're not interested in how the healings happen anymore?
Tobiah: Eh!
Me: Yeah, right.
Tobiah: Tell me, don't tell me – whatever.
Jesus: Cool!
Saul: So; Ezra's?
Me: What did you say, Saul?
Saul: Ezra's?
Me: What?
Saul: Ezra's?
Me: Where?

Saul tackled me and tried to drill his knuckle into the middle of my chest (which really hurts), then Tobiah tried to do the same to him. Jesus said, "Hey, guys, why don't we go to Ezra's?" so we chased him all the way to Ezra's.

Turns out Ezra was over at Eli's. Saul said, "so; Eli's?" so we chased him to Eli's.

Because we were already running, and Eli's dad said to go on in, we burst into Eli's room. They were sitting on the floor playing mancala (that board game you play with pebbles), but they both shrunk back when we busted in. Eli yelled out, "Whoa! Where's the fuckin fire?" Tobiah jumped on him and tried to do the knuckle thing on his chest, and so Saul jumped on Ezra and did the same to him. They were all laughing and yelling, so I grabbed Jesus and drilled my knuckle into his chest. But he just stood there.

"Oh! Right!" Jesus said, and then he buckled like he really felt it. "Ah, stop!" he said, unconvincingly.

"Dude, forget it."

"No, go ahead."

"You can't even feel it!"

"No, go ahead, I just wasn't paying attention."

Eli's dad stuck his head in the door. "Boys! Settle down. If you need something to do, there's wood to chop." His answer to everything.

We all stopped and Eli said, "okay, Dad, it's cool."

Once Eli's dad left, Saul said, "Ezra, feel like cooking?"

Ezra: No, not really. We *were* in the middle of a game, but *someone* knocked the board over.

Saul: Great, so you're free!

Eli: Hey, where's Oren?

Me: Guess.

Eli: Oh, right. Man, he is so lucky.

Ezra: Don't worry Eli, you'll find someone.

Eli: I'm not *worried*.

Tobiah: You guys sure look all chummy.

Eli: Yeah, so?

Tobiah: I'm just saying.

I took that opportunity to punch Jesus in the shoulder.

"Huh?" Jesus said, like I'd only tapped him on the shoulder.

"You don't feel anything?" I asked.

"Sure I do," he said.

"Like what?" Tobiah asked.

"Well, I'm kinda ticklish," Jesus answered.

"Oh, reeeaaaally," Ezra said.

Three seconds later we were all tickling Jesus, and he was laughing his head off.

Three minutes later we were all chopping wood. But it was worth it.

2:10

I was walking back to my house from the market. It was my turn to cook dinner and I had a hankering for fish. Maybe I was thinking of Nissa, I don't know. The sun was at its most golden and a soft breeze had kicked up. Jesus came running up to me.
"Joel, she liked it!"
"Who liked what? I asked.
"Dara! She liked the flower I carved for her! You were right!"
"Of course I'm right! You kind of waited a long time."
"Do you think she got that I like her?"
"If she has a brain."
"So what do I do next?"
"Umm, I don't know. Ask her to go for a walk."
"Yeah! Good idea."
"Hey, Jesus. Have you thought this through? I mean, if you *are* a prophet, can you like, kiss her and stuff?
"Why wouldn't I?"
"And didn't you mention that your dad was against you dating?"
"I'll fall off that bridge when I come to it."

"Jesus, there could be a lot at stake here."
"It's funny, you look just like Joel, but you sound just like Tobiah. Or the old Tobiah, anyway."
"Just looking out for you."

Jesus thought a moment. "God is love, right?"
"So you've said."
"Well… that's what I'm looking for, right?"
"Ha! I guess. But what happens… "
"Joel, relax. You're thinking too hard."
"It's funny, you look just like Jesus, but you sound just like Eli. Or the old Eli, anyway."
"Jesus, the ladies' man. I like the sound of that."

The next day we're all hanging out by the river, except for Tobiah. Only this time Jesus was completely bummed cause his dad had just bawled him out for spending time with Dara, and then his mom tried to stick up for him and things went south from there.
I asked him, "so why is your dad so paranoid?"
"He's afraid about what will happen when I start doing the prophet stuff."
"Why?"
"Because before, people got weirded out by it. That's why we left Egypt. So now I'm supposed to just wait."
"For what?" I asked.
"I don't know, a sign or something. Till I'm ready to be the Messiah."
Ezra said, "wait, Messiah? I thought you were just a prophet."

At that exact moment, Tobiah comes walking up and from out of nowhere gives Jesus this big shove.

"Tobiah!" Jesus says, "what is the deal?"

"You have to have everything, is that it?" he says, his teeth all clenched.

"What are you talking about?" Jesus asked, looking around at us for help.

Saul steps up. "Dude, what's going on?"

"Because of you and your stupid carvings, she broke up with me," Tobiah says.

"Who?" Saul asks.

"Who do you think? Dara!" Tobiah yells.

Jesus just closes his eyes, drops his head and turns away.

Tobiah yells, "Hey, I'm talking to you!"

Eli takes Tobiah by the shoulders, "Hey, enough, tough guy. Let's try talking this out, okay?"

Tobiah throws him off and says, "Shut up, Eli."

Saul stares at his brother and says, "who *are* you?"

"Me?" Tobiah says, "*me*? I'm the guy that Jesus has set out to make my life miserable!" Yeah, doesn't really work as a sentence, but it's clear he's mad as hell.

Ezra says from behind Eli, "Jesus would never hurt anyone."

"Oh, yeah?" Tobiah goes, still yelling. "He took away my *God*, he took away who I *am*, and now he takes away my *girl*. Why do *you* get it all?

Why you? You're this oddball nobody and you're a lousy prophet and a terrible person and no friend of mine. Or anybody!"

This was a whole new role for Tobiah. He sure had the passion for it, even if he was struggling with the words. After his verbal bitchslap to Jesus, he stormed away, which was probably good, cause Jesus could have taken him easily. Not that he would have hurt him. But a carpenter's son beats a scholarly bag-maker's son any day.

Saul looked at us and shrugged and followed after Tobiah. Oren followed, too.
Ezra came around to face Jesus. "Are you alright?"
"I didn't know," Jesus said.
Eli said, "Tobiah's just worked up. He'll calm down."

It wasn't until that moment that I remembered how mad I'd gotten at Jesus awhile back. I was kind of embarrassed. Tobiah had looked pretty foolish, and I wondered if I'd looked the same, or if Jesus was thinking about it, too. I guess I was being pretty self-centered thinking that way. I mean, I felt bad for Jesus, but since I'd done the same thing to him, I felt like an idiot. Jesus looked up at me. I always forget about that damn mind-reading thing.
"I'm sorry," was all I could think of to say.
Jesus said, "so is this what my life is going to be like? Pissing people off no matter what I do?"

And then the weirdest thing happened. I still get goosebumps just thinking about it. The sun disappeared behind a cloud, a really thick one, and the wind picked up, and it was like all of a sudden we were about to be swallowed up by a storm. It looked like this big black cloud was close enough to touch. "Oh, crap." Eli said. It started to sprinkle, and Jesus yells up to the sky, "I GIVE UP!" There was a crack of lightning and all of a sudden it was all gone. The sun was shining, the breeze was soft and the birds slowly started singing again. All that took as much time as it takes to tell.

Ezra said, "Oh. My. Was that really... God?"
Jesus dropped to his knees and started crying. We knelt down and put a hand on his shoulders. Even Eli.
After awhile, he stood up and said. "Excuse me, I need to be alone now. Thanks."
And with that, he vanished.

Eli said, "*man,* that is cool. I wish I could do that."
Ezra said, "did he really say 'messiah'?"
I said, "poor guy."

Part Three

3:1

I was starting to get worried about Jesus. It had been hours since he'd vanished. Again. I didn't feel like waiting for his folks to come sniffing for answers this time, so I decided to go find him. Where would he go? Last time he said he was aiming for home and wound up in Joppa. So he could be anywhere. Like, *any*where!

I figured he didn't go home – he'd just had an argument with his dad about dating Dara, and then got busted by Tobiah for stealing his girl. But I don't think Jesus knew about them being a couple, or he wouldn't have started up with her. If there was a dog house around, I would have looked there, cause that's kinda where he was already. And then the whole sky craziness. And now it was clouding up again and looking like rain. It made me nervous.

Then it came to me – Jesus was up in the hills. It made perfect sense! It's where he was usually tromping around, figuring out what it means to be a prophet in this crazy-ass world we live in. I was tempted to go check in on Tobiah, but I figured Saul and Oren had that covered.

So off I went up into the hills, thinking back on my friendship with Jesus: didn't really know him, mad as hell at him, willing to tolerate him, felt sorry for him, tried to help him, became friends with him, watched him disappear. Whether or not he is a prophet or even a messiah, I like the guy. He loves the sea just like I do. And he needs a friend. We could both do worse.

I was huffing and puffing from charging up the path so fast, and when I got to this one point that overlooks Nazareth, there he was, sitting cross-legged on a big rock. I came up behind him slowly. "Been here long?" I asked.

He didn't seem surprised that I was there, and didn't turn around.

"Hi, Joel. I'm not sure how long I've been here."

"Does your butt hurt?" I asked him. "Cause if you've been here awhile…"

"Thanks for answering my call."

"Huh?" I said. "I didn't hear anything."

"You're here, aren't you?"

"Yeah, but that's cause… ." I could feel the hair on my arms rising.

"Don't worry, it's still me," he said.

"I'm not worried," I lied.

He finally turned around, smiling at me.

"So," I asked, "what the hell happened?"

"Whoo, boy, where do I start?" He paused. "I had a little chat with the Father."

"THE Father? As in… "

"Yeah. *That* One."

"Was He pissed?"

Jesus chuckled. "Yes. And no. There is frighteningly tremendous power - but it's all good."

"So… ?"

"So, I think we have an understanding."

"Care to share that with a mere mortal?"

He smiled again. "I get to be me. At least for now."

"So you're not a prophet?"

"Joel, don't tell anyone, but I'm the Messiah. Or will be."

"No fucking way! Oh, sorry, damn! Oh, sorry again." Jesus laughed. "And you can be you, too."

"Yeah, but I just cussed in front of the… seriously, the Messiah? THE Messiah?"

"Stop. I'm Jesus, and that's how you should treat me. Don't worry about the other stuff."

"But then you shouldn't have told me!"

"I wanted you to know, but nobody else. He said you could handle it."

"*He* said? Really? Wow!"

"Yeah, so don't tell the other guys or you'll piss Him off."

"Shit. Oh, crap, I did it again!"

Jesus shook his head. "You're hopeless."

"Yeah, well. I've got a Messiah looking after me, so I guess I'll be okay."

"Lucky for you," he said. I was hoping he'd smile then, but he didn't.

"So how exactly do you plan on freeing us. From the Romans and stuff?"

"Oh, there's much more to be freed of than that."

"Really?"

"Verily."

"So the Messiah has been prophesied for… I don't know, a gazillon years, and you're it?"

"Yes. Nice to meet you."

I noticed the clouds had gotten really dark and were blocking the sunset.

"We should head back down in case there's lightening," I said.

"I'll take care of it," he said. And right then, the clouds slowly crept back into themselves and after a minute or two, the sky was clear.

"Damn!" I said. "That was pretty impressive. Show-off."

"No, I'm not allowed to show off. I did it to make sure you were safe getting back down."

"So now I owe you?"

"No. You and I will always be even. Okay? Those are the rules; you don't tell, I don't show off, we're always even. Deal?"

I had a bad feeling I should have thought a lot longer about this, but I said it anyway: "deal."

There was still a good breeze on our way back down, and it was the weirdest thing, but I thought I kept hearing the wind say, "thank you." So, I figure now maybe I'm crazy, too.

On the way back down from the hills, Jesus and I decided to meet at the well after dinner. We figured the other guys might show up, too and we could get an update on Tobiah and all.

When I got home, Ezra and Eli were there.

"See, Ezra, he's right here," Eli said. "I told you not to worry."

"Where *were* you, we thought you'd disappeared, too!" Ezra said.

"Have you seen Jesus?" Ezra asked.

"Yeah, he's fine," I said. I could see more questions coming, but I didn't know how to head them off.

"Where was he? Is he okay? Did he say anything about being the Messiah? Where is he now?" Ezra splurted out.

"He's fine. He's home. I found him up in the hills." I said.

Eli said, "cool. Good news. I'm off to dinner."

Ezra rolled his eyes. As Eli walked off, he said, "Hey, let's meet at the well after dinner!" Then he turned back to me and said, "I swear that guy will never get enough food. Are you okay?" Ezra asked.

"Yeah!" I said a little too enthusiastically.

"You sure?" he said, giving me a funny look.

"Yep, right as rain! Well, I should probably get inside. See ya tonight!" Again with my peppy voice.

I didn't say much at dinner. My dad never talks much while he eats, so it was fine. Until he said, "do you need me to tie a few knots in a rope for you to untangle? You look like you've got a lot on your mind."

I let out a big sigh. Crap, what a dead giveaway!

"I'm fine," I said. "It's just typical teenage stuff."

"Girls?" my dad said.

"Well, sort of," I lied.

"What lucky girl do you have your eye on?" he asked.

"Who, me? Oh, um, no one really." And then I thought about Nissa from Caesarea. The firelight in her eyes and her little wave.

"Hmm," my dad said, "I'm not sure I believe you. You've got that look in your eyes."

"I do?" I was stunned. I didn't realize there was such a look, or that I would have it thinking of Nissa.

"Joel, your mother used to say, 'where your treasure lies, your heart will point the way.' "

"No kidding. That's good."

"Yes, I think so, too. She also said a number of other things like, 'for the love of God, please stop leaving your clothes on the floor,' but I think I like the heart one best."

Dads can be surprisingly funny sometimes.

3:2

Saul told me that after Tobiah stormed away from the rest of us, he and Oren followed him to Dara's house. Tobiah was about to make a big scene, but they dragged him away before he made too much of a stink. Back at the twins' house, their mom got involved and said all Tobiah needed was a good meal, so she whipped something up and Saul and Oren ate it all cause Tobiah was too distraught to eat. (That's a good word, distraught.) It took Oren and Saul all night to calm him down, and even after dinner he refused to go to the well to meet up with the rest of us.

That night at the well...

Oren: Jesus, you need to go talk to Tobiah. He thinks you stole his girlfriend.

Jesus: Seriously, I had no idea. Ask Joel!

Me: Yep.

Saul: All I know is, ever since the trip to Caesarea, he has not been the same.

Jesus: He said he was okay with everything! He said he felt better!

Ezra: He's clearly in denial.

Jesus: Okay, so what do I say? I mean, other than I'm sorry. And I'd just like to point out that, for the record, that is not an easy thing for me to say.

Eli: Suck it up, big man. Happens to the best of us.

Ezra: It's a good thing Tobiah wasn't there for the whole weather weirdness.

Oren: Say what?

Ezra: Oh, that's right, you guys had left. Yeah, this huge cloud came down…

Jesus: Umm, hey so, what were you just saying Joel?

Oren: Yeah, come to think of it, there was some weird weather going on. What does that have to do with… Jesus? Was that you?

Me: No, that wasn't him.

Ezra: Oh, come on!

Jesus: It wasn't! Oh, shoot, here comes Tobiah.

Tobiah came walking up slowly.

Tobiah: Guys. Jesus.

All of us: Hey.

Jesus: Tobiah, I had *no* idea you were seeing Dara.

Tobiah thought about that awhile. "Yeah, okay."

Jesus: Yeah? Really?

Tobiah: I still kinda hate your guts, but I've never known you to lie before.

Ezra: You know, Tobiah, passion is not a bad look on you.

Tobiah: Yeah, whatever.

Jesus: Have you talked to her?

Tobiah: Yeah. She wants to talk to you.

Eli: Uh-oh!

Saul: Go easy, big man.

Me: God go with you.

Jesus: Oh thanks, I would never have thought of that.

Saul started laughing, not exactly sure why.

Jesus grabbed my sleeve. "C'mon, you're going with me."

They watched us walk off.

Tobiah said, "what's the deal with everyone? First Ezra and Eli, and now Jesus and Joel."

Saul said "Don't worry little brother – you still got me, man!" and he tried to snuggle under Tobiah's arm.

Tobiah said, "One, you're my twin; two, I'm taller than you; and three, get away from me."

They wound up wrestling, and then Oren jumped in. That's what Saul told me anyway.

As we're walking through town, Jesus says, "okay, climb up in your tree and I'll bring her over here."

"You *want* me to eavesdrop?" I asked.

"Well, yeah. In case I mess up. Let me know when I get off track."

"And how will I do that with Dara right there?"

"Believe me, Joel, if something big goes on in your head, I'll hear it."

"Hmm, great" I said as I climbed up.

A few minutes later, Dara and Jesus came walking up.

Dara: So I heard Tobiah was pretty mad at you.

Jesus: Yeah, but I think he's okay now. I honestly did not know you were seeing him.

Dara: We just talked a couple of times, but it wasn't that big a deal.

Jesus: I guess he thought it was.

Dara: I guess. So you're still interested?

Jesus: Well, I don't know. I kind of have this rule that I try to treat people the way I'd like them to treat me.

Dara: Yeah, so…

Jesus: So I wouldn't want be mean to my friend Tobiah.

Dara: Wait. What?

Jesus: If I thought someone had stolen a girl from me, I'd want them to step back.

Dara: But you didn't *steal* me from him. I *chose* you.

Jesus: Oh.

Dara: So wait, you thought if you stepped back, you could just point me back toward Tobiah and all would be well?

Jesus: I'm thinking I should say no to that?

Dara: What kind of ditz do you think I am? Or do you think that I'm so desperate, that I'd just pick up with any guy who comes calling?

Jesus: I don't think you're a ditz, I think you're really…

Dara: And what about this personal rule of yours?
How about how *I* feel?
Jesus: Uhhh…
Dara: Shouldn't you respect my wishes and go out
with me, because that's what you'd want me to do
for you?

I was trying to mentally signal Jesus to just stop
talking, but I didn't seem to be getting through. So I
tried dropping an acorn on his head.

Jesus: Ow!
Dara: What now?
Jesus: I just got hit by an acorn.
Dara: Don't try to change the subject.
Jesus: You're a lot smarter than I thought you were.
Dara: So you *do* think I'm a ditz!
Jesus: No, I mean, I knew you were smart, I just…
Dara: Jesus, look, I like you. And I really like the
carved blossom.
Jesus: I like you, too.

He and I both checked the sky for stray lightening.
Dara stepped closer to Jesus and wrapped her arms
around his waist.

Dara whispered, "so what about Tobiah?
Jesus said "who?"

3:3

After about a week, things seemed to have settled down (pretty much), so we all pitched in to have Ezra make another dinner for us. He said we each had to bring a flower made out of something other than wood, as kind of a joke on Jesus' gift the last time.

Oren wanted to bring Leah, but then Jesus thought about bringing Dara, and then it got to be this big deal, so we said no girls. Social stuff gets so complicated; I'm not sure why people even bother. Give me a relaxed dinner by the beach any day. Which makes me think about Nissa. I liked her sense of humor. I wonder if she already has a boyfriend? Oh well. I mean, if I don't know for sure, why get myself all worked up, right? Believe me, I have *not* forgotten about the sea.

When we got to Ezra's house, Eli was already there helping cook, which kinda made everyone's eyebrows shoot up. I guess he wasn't very good though, because Ezra kept sighing and buzzing around and his voice kept getting higher and higher.

First, we shared our flower-like things. Tobiah brought a pine cone, Oren brought a stack of leaves that he had impaled with a nail, and Saul had taken a bunch of fishtails and tied them together with twine, which actually looked pretty cool. Unfortunately, it smelled terrible.

Eli brought an actual flower, which we all thought was cheating, but Ezra topped us all by making blossoms out of beets as part of the meal. I brought a rock that I'd tried to chisel into a blossom, but it looked more like something had just chewed on it.

Then we ate like men.

Me: We've had quite a year, guys.
Saul: And our little Oren is all growed up and getting married!
Tobiah: Saul, what is the deal with calling everyone little?
Ezra: It's a term of endearment, right?
Saul: No, I just think of you guys as my little brothers.
Eli: Are you nuts? You're the little brother around here.
Saul just smiled.

Tobiah: I sure never expected to see Ezra and Eli hanging out together.
Eli wrapped his arm around Ezra's neck and rubbed his head with his knuckles. "He's my boyee!"
Ezra just smiled.

Oren: I am gonna miss hanging out with you guys.
Me: What are you talking about! We live in the same dinky town, you're gonna see us all the time!
Oren: No, I don't think so. I'm gonna be with my misses, every chance I get.
Saul: Really? Well that kinda sucks. No offense.
Tobiah: What did you think, Saul, that we would all be around forever?

Saul: No. Well, yeah.

Oren: Some day, Saul, you'll settle down and you'll understand.

Ezra: A toast to Oren and Leah!

The rest of us: To Oren and Leah!

Ezra: So who do you think is next?

Saul: Jesus! Oh, sorry, Tobiah.

Jesus: Guys, Dara and I *just* started seeing each other.

Eli: Wait till she finds out you're a prophet: sexy!

Jesus: Yeah, ha ha.

Me: Pass the bread.

Tobiah: I may not be getting married soon, but I'm not staying around here much longer.

Eli: Yeah, whatever. Where are you gonna go?

Tobiah just looked down at his food.

Oren stands and says: I'd like to make a toast to all you guys. You are my friends, I don't have any others, and I wouldn't have it any other way. To you guys.

The rest of us: To you guys!

Tobiah: To adventures, past and future!

The rest of us: To adventures, past and future.

It was a nice, relaxed evening, like we had the whole world out in front of us. But that changed pretty quickly.

Ezra, Eli, Jesus and I were hanging out at the river the next day, just watching the current and throwing stuff into it, when Saul came walking up all frantic.

Saul: Guys!

Eli: Hey, what's with you?

Saul: Tobiah's gone!

Jesus: What? Gone?

Saul: Yeah! Last night he asked my dad for his share of whatever Dad was going to leave us, and then took off this morning.

Me: No way!

Eli: Son of a bitch! He owed me money!

Ezra: Did he say where he was going?

Saul: No. My dad made him promise to think about it for a few days, but he got up early this morning and took off.

Me: He didn't even say goodbye.

Ezra: Did *you* get to say goodbye, Saul?

Saul: Sort of. Last night we talked till we fell asleep, like usual. It's weird. I've been with him my whole life. Every single day. And now he's gone.

We all just kind of sat there, numb. Sure, Saul must have felt it most, but it was strange. Tobiah could have just been home instead of with us, and it should have felt the same. But this was like, permanent.

Eli: So how much did he get?

Ezra: Eli, c'mon!

Eli: What?

Jesus: Oh, man. I feel terrible.

Saul: I think he would have done it eventually anyway.

Jesus: Really?

Saul: Yeah, I could tell he was already pretty fed up with the religious stuff. I heard the Rabbi complaining to my dad that Tobiah had been kind of a smart ass to him lately, so I could tell he wasn't into it anymore. And from what you said, Dara really wasn't into him, either.

Jesus: Yeah, but he *left*.

Eli: He even talked about it last night! I honestly didn't think he had it in him.

Me: Yeah, you're right. I didn't think anything of it.

Jesus: It was like a farewell party.

Eli: I wonder where he's headed.

Ezra: Saul, let us know if you need anything.

Me: Yeah. We're *all* your brothers.

Saul: Thanks, guys. But you're not him.

That night, Saul asked if I would sleep over at his house cause he couldn't face going to sleep alone. I honestly don't get why I'm the go-to guy for everyone, but whatever. It was also a little awkward to sleep in Tobiah's bed, like I was the new Tobiah or something. Or a temporary one, at least.

Once the lamp went out, we just lay there. Saul finally broke the silence.

Saul: So how was your day?

Me: Uhh, okay. How was your day?

Saul: Seriously?

Me: Oh, right. Pretty crappy, I guess.

Saul: Yeah. Thanks for being here.

Me: Sure.

Saul: Why do you think he left?

Me: I don't know. I guess he wasn't very happy with the way things were going. With Jesus and all.

Saul: Yeah.

Me: What?

Saul: You don't think it was cause of me, do you?

Me: No! Why would you think that?

Saul: I don't know. Maybe he was tired of me or something.

Me: Saul, I've known you for a long time, and I've never once gotten tired of you.

Saul: Yeah? Cool. I still think Tobiah might have been. Think about it. Every day, same brother.

Me: Saul, you're going to drive yourself crazy thinking like that. If you don't know for sure, why get worked up?

Saul: Think he'll ever come back?

Me: Sure.

Saul: Really? When?

Me: When his money runs out.

Saul: Ha! Yeah. Yeah, I like that. G'night Joel.

Me: G'night, Saul.

3:4

Jesus and I had gotten into the habit of meeting in the late afternoon to climb up in the hills and talk and stuff. He usually does most of the talking. Well one day, I can't find him, so I decide to go by myself. When I get to the bottom of the path, there he is, coming down with Dara. Awkward.

Jesus says, "oh hey, Joel! Going for a hike?"

I say, "well, yeah. Hey, Dara."

Dara gives Jesus a look and says, "hi, Joel."

Jesus looks at Dara, then at me, blinks and says, "oh, were we supposed to… oh, dude, I'm sorry, I just…"

"No," I say, "it's fine. A hike is a hike, right?"

Dara speaks up. "Jesus, why don't you go back up with Joel, and I'll head back to town."

She's a sweet girl, and smart.

"You're sure?" Jesus asks.

"Yeah, no, it's fine," she says. She gives his hand a squeeze and heads off. "Later, guys!"

Jesus just stands and watches her go.

"Jesus."

"Huh, yeah?" he says.

"Man, you are smitten with a capital Smit!"

He laughs. "She's pretty great. Smart as a whip, too. I always feel like I'm about two steps behind."

"You don't have to go up again if you don't want to," I say, giving him an out.

"No, I'm ready! Let's go."

We hiked for a while, and then he said, "sorry I forgot about meeting today. I swear, when I'm with Dara, it's like the rest of the world disappears."

I kind of hated to remind him of the prophet and/or messiah thing, but what with Tobiah gone, I went for it. "Jesus, how does this all work with, you know, your 'mission'."

He sluffed it off, "oh Joel. I'm young, I'm healthy. I've got plenty of time to worry about that later."

"Have you told her?" I asked.

"Are you kidding? She'd think I was crazy."

"Well, don't you have to tell her *some*time?"

He stopped walking and looked out at the view.

"This is just for now," he said. "It won't last."

"How do you know?"

Jesus sighed. "Because it can't. But for now, I'm going to live. That was the deal, remember? I get to be me."

I glanced up at the sky, but it seemed pretty quiet, so either God was taking a break, or it really was okay.

"Okay. Just be careful," I said, sounding more like a dad than a friend.

Jesus looked back at me and smiled, then opened his arms to the sky and let out this big whoop.

"You really like her, huh?" I asked.

"YES!" he yelled down to Nazareth.

On the way back down, he said, "do you think I'm making a mistake?"

I thought about that, and then I told him about my mom's saying that my dad had told me the other night. About how your heart leads you to where your real treasure is.

"Yes!" Jesus said, turning around to look at me. "Exactly!"

When I got back home, Dara was there waiting for me.

"Hi, Joel!" she said.

"Hey, Dara! Jesus went home."

"Yeah, I wanted to talk to you, actually."

Uh-oh. "Sure," I said.

"You're like Jesus' best friend, right?"

"I guess. Yeah."

"Well, is it just me, or is he a bit quirky sometimes?"

"Quirky? Like how?" No flies on me.

"I don't know. Kind of distracted. A little nervous. Keeps looking up at the sky like it's about to fall."

"Heh, heh, oh that Jesus. He's sure a great guy."

"Hmm. I can see why you guys get along."

"Well, if that's all, I kinda have to…"

"Wait. Does he ever say anything about me? Because I really like him."

My heart hit the dirt. "Yes."

"Care to share?"

Luckily, I suddenly realized what I could say. "He really, *really* likes you."

She smiled. "Cool. You guys – it's so hard to get anything out of you. I'll see you later. Thanks!"

"Yeah, mm-hmm, bye!"

Whew!

I went in to help my dad fix dinner. He had some big news for me.

"Was that little Dara?" he asked. "She's growing into quite a lovely little lady."

"Dad." I said. "She's dating Jesus."

"Oh," he said. "Well, things can change!"

"We live in Nazareth, remember?"

"Things can change even in Nazareth. For instance, I have some news."

"Yeah?"

"Yes. Remember me telling you that the husband of your mother's cousin died recently?

Well, your mother's cousin is coming to Nazareth for a visit."

"Here? What for?" I asked.

"Well, to visit me," he said. "Us, in a way."

The idea slowly dawned on me. We kept working on dinner, but my thoughts were whizzing around like swallows at sunset. A potential new mom. Not even a *new* mom, since I could barely remember my mom. A potential new wife. He was lonely. I wasn't around much anymore. I felt bad. And scared. A new person in this little house? What was she like? Would they even want me around? Were they going to have sex (eww!) and kids (ugh!) and…?

"She's coming next week. Are you okay with that?"

"Sure, Dad. It's fine."

"I met her once years and years ago at my wedding. And I hear good things about her."

"Great," I said. "I'll look forward to it."

The rest of dinner was very quiet.

3:5

Okay, I admit I wasn't there for the first part, but here's how it went down as far as I can piece together.

The other night, Ezra was at the well, waiting for Eli to walk over with him to the field where we were all meeting. Eli is pretty much always late, so Ezra didn't think anything of it. He was looking down at the ground when he saw a bunch of shadows gather around him.

He looked up and it was Mordecai and his goons, the same guys who'd beat him up way back.

Mordecai: Hey, Ezra. Where are your buddies?
Ezra: They're on their way.
Mordecai: Really.
Ezra: Yes, really. Go away.
Mordecai: Word has it you've been busy.
Ezra: What's that supposed to mean?
Mordecai: It's bad enough that you sniff around us guys, but now you have a real live boyfriend.
Ezra: You don't know anything.
Mordecai: Oh, I beg to differ. See, the Torah says we should stone homos like you. You're a bomination.
Ezra: The word is "abomination," dumb-ass.
Mordecai: Whatever. We've always known exactly what you are. So, it's our civic, no our *sacred* duty to take care of some unfinished business.
Ezra stood up. "And who are you to go around deciding things? Just because you have a gang to help you with your dirty work, doesn't mean you have the right…"
Mordecai shoved him down against the well.
Mordecai: You'd know all about dirty work wouldn't you.

Right then, Eli came walking up. Eli likes to talk big, but I've noticed he rarely acts on it.

Eli: Get away from him, asshole.
Mordecai: Lookie here, fellas! His boyfriend arrives, just in the nick of time.
Eli went to help Ezra up, but they blocked his way.

Eli: Get the hell out of my way.

Mordecai: Or what? You gonna do a little faggot dance for us?

Eli: Come on, Ezra, let's get out of here.

Mordecai: You and your little boyfriend aren't going anywhere. C'mon, boys, let's find some place more private.

There were six of them, so they pushed Eli and Ezra down the street and behind a crumbling old wall. Eli and Ezra stood side by side facing them, their literal backs to the wall.

Eli: You're making a big mistake.

Mordecai: No, we actually made a big mistake in not taking care of this punk the first time around.

Eli: He's never done anything to you.

Mordecai: See, that's where you're wrong. He's turning this whole town gay. Look at you. It was bad enough when you used to be a skinny little prick, but now you're a skinny little fag, and that's something we just can't put up with.

Eli: Fuck you.

Mordecai: No, Eli. I think *you're* the one who's fucked.

The goons bent down to pick up rocks and pieces of the crumbled wall.

Mordecai: As members of the town of Nazareth, I find you guilty, and sentence you to death by
        stoning.

Eli turned his back to them and grabbed Ezra and pinned him against the wall. "Stay behind me," he said in Ezra's ear. Ezra fought to get around Eli and take his share of the hits, but Eli wouldn't let him. Mordecai started the throwing, and they kept going till Eli's blood was showing through his robe. Ezra couldn't think of anything else to do, so he started yelling for help.

It took a while before someone came running up, we're not sure who, and yelled at them to stop, and when others showed up, too, the gang ran off. No one was too happy about what they found.

Someone went for the town Elders, someone else ran to get Ezra and Eli's parents. Saul and I were walking back from the fields since no one
else had shown up, and we heard the yelling so we went to see what was going on. Eli's head had been hit a bunch of times, and he was bleeding pretty badly. Ezra kept yelling even though people were trying to calm him down.

Saul and I looked at each other and immediately started running for Jesus' house. We found him in his courtyard, trying to show Dara how to whittle, and when he saw the looks on our faces he knew something was up.

The four of us ran back, and they had moved Eli into an old barn with only half a roof. His parents were there, and pretty soon the town
Elders showed up, too, and everyone was talking softly and intensely, like arrow shot whispers.

Eli's dad saw me, and came towards me crying. "Go say goodbye." The Elders kind of shooed people away so we could have a few last words with Eli.

Saul, Jesus, Dara and I walked over. Eli was barely conscious, and he looked really pale. Ezra was kneeling next to him, his bloody hand on Eli's shoulder. There were just a few torches for light, so it was a pretty surreal scene. When Ezra saw Jesus, he started crying. Jesus put his hand on Ezra's head and said, "don't be afraid." But then he looked down at Eli and saw how bad he looked. The light hit Jesus' face, and I have to say he didn't look real fearless himself. He glanced up at me and his face relaxed like he was recognizing me or something.

Then he knelt down next to Eli. I'm not sure when he'd first put it there, but I was suddenly aware of Saul's hand on my shoulder. I could see his eyes, squinting, like he could barely watch. It occurred to me that Saul might not make it through losing another one of us. It was all in slow motion. I could hear some women quietly wailing over by the crowd.

I didn't know what to do. I trusted Jesus, but I felt completely helpless. I wondered what Jesus was thinking. I thought about how he'd said that God doesn't make people die. And that there was more life. And how God is like your family holding you. I thought of my dad, and I suddenly felt like it was a good idea for him to get married again. And Tobiah and how I wished him well, wherever the hell he was. And oddly enough, I thought of the Roman soldier I'd pegged with the egg, and all the folks we'd met in Caesarea, and the woman who'd given us breakfast, and the sea and the way it sparkles like gold, and the firelight in Nissa's eyes, and I looked up at the sky, at the dark and the stars, and somehow it all seemed so *beautiful*. All of it. And I somehow knew in that moment that everything would be okay, no matter what happened. It was really going to be okay.

Oren had just arrived and I felt his big arms going around me and Saul's shoulders. And then I saw Jesus look over at me, and he had this incredible look on his face. Blissful, I'd call it.

Then Eli started to stir. I looked down at him, and he looked fine. Like he was just waking up.
"What the hell?" he said.
Ezra said, "Eli? How do you feel?"
"Not bad. What are you guys doing here? Where… ? Oh. Oh, yeah. Ezra, are you okay?"
"Yes," Ezra laughed with relief, "I'm fine. We were all so worried about you."
Eli looked at Jesus. "Huh. I feel like I should be thanking you."
Jesus said, "Can you get up?"
Eli slowly got up, and he felt the back of this head. His hand came back sticky with blood.
"Gross," he said. "But I guess my noggin is still in one piece."

That was when the crowd started to notice what was going on. I happened to look over at Dara and she was wide-eyed and trembling, so I took her hand.

She blinked and leaned into me. The crowd came in like a gentle wave and everyone started talking when they saw Eli alive and well. We were all swept to the back, and I saw Jesus walk out of the barn. Dara dropped my hand and followed him.

Once Eli had washed the blood off his head and Ezra had washed the blood off his hands, they were perfectly fine, not a scratch. The town called it a miracle. I don't think anyone linked it to Jesus, since only the five of us were there when he healed him. Well, and Dara.

Mordecai and his gang were hauled in front of the Elders and there was a special town meeting where everyone argued and yelled and cried and tried to figure out what they should do. It was finally decided that the six guys should scrub the temple floor every day (except the Sabbath) for a whole year, rebuild the wall with the bricks they'd used, and meet with the rabbis once a week. And if they tried to get back at anyone, they'd have to leave town. For good.

I guess they talked to Ezra, too, but he never told us what happened there. And it turns out it wasn't just Eli's head that was healed. But you'll see.

3:6

The next day I was talking to Jesus. It was late morning, and there was a nice breeze blowing as we walked towards the river.

"So, how did it feel?" I asked. "Healing Eli, I mean."
"Good. Odd. At first, I was kind of worried, cause I haven't done it in so long and Eli looked pretty bad. But then..."
"Yeah?"
"I don't know – I looked at you, and it was like... I don't know. It was just very reassuring. Not like... I mean... it reminded me of my whole arrangement with God. And that I could trust that. As much as I trust you. I guess."

Wow. The Messiah (well, maybe) trusts me! *Me!* Then again, he could just be seriously self-deluded. Does it matter? My friend really trusts me. Hard to feel bad about *that* news.

"Yeah, but how did it feel? Like, what happens?" I asked.
Jesus paused. "It's incredible. It's like... endless light... and profound peace and the universe singing and... it's kinda like that day on the beach in Caesaria. Only times ten - no, times a hundred!"
"So you should be feeling pretty good," I said.
"I should. Except Dara was kinda freaked out about it."
"Kinda?"

"Well, more than kinda." He sighed. "Why is there always *some*one who isn't happy? I mean, you'd think everyone would be pretty satisfied with the results. But they never are."

"I think you did an amazing job! Not just for Eli, but for Ezra, Saul, me, the whole freakin' town! Think about what would have happened if we'd lost Eli."

"Thanks, Joel," Jesus said. "It's still tough with Dara. She wanted to run around telling everyone it was me. When I told her she couldn't tell anyone, she asked me who I really am, and I didn't feel like I could explain it."

"So what *did* you tell her?" I asked.

"That I have certain abilities and I don't understand the full extent of them."

"Hmm."

"What?"

"I think you *do* know the full extent of your powers, even if you haven't used them completely, and, *and* the full ramifications of them."

"And you get on my case for reading *your* mind! Oye."

"How are your folks doing with it?"

"Oh, man. I think they're still shaking.

 "Did they say anything?"

"My dad started to, but I told him I'm the freakin' messiah, I can do whatever I want."

"No way!"

"No, not really. Sometimes I'd like to, though. They're happy about Eli, but they don't like that other people might find out it was me, cause then all the questions start. I don't really blame them. Raising a kid is hard enough, but they have no idea how to raise a messiah. Sometimes it feels like there's so much pressure in my house, the walls are about to blow out. So I didn't dare tell them about Dara."

"And how did it end with Dara?"

"She's going to think about it."

"Oooo," I said, "Not a great sign."

"No, not at all," Jesus said.

"Well," I said, "you never know."

"It's bound to end sooner or later. But I would definitely prefer later."

Later that afternoon I was feeling fidgety about everything. Eli almost died, Ezra still seemed kind of skittish, Saul was slowly coming out of the dumps from his brother leaving town, and Oren wasn't around all that much anymore. Plus, Zelda, my dead mom's cousin was coming to visit soon. *Zelda!* What kind of a name is that? I was still happy for my dad, but wondered what it meant for me.

I got so jittery, I decided to walk over to Jesus'. Turns out Eli was there.

"Eli, what's up?" I asked.

"Jesus helped me make a new cutting board for Ezra."

"Say again?"

"Jesus helped… you heard me."

They'd taken different kinds of wood to make it striped. "Wow," I said. "That's pretty cool."

"Well, Jesus did most of it," Eli said.

"You're actually pretty good with wood," Jesus said. "Ever think of becoming a carpenter?"

"My dad would kill me. I am a sandal-makers son, and it's a sandal-maker's life that I will lead."

It was the first time I'd ever heard Eli say much about his future.

Eli continued, "Thanks, Jesus. I couldn't have done this without you." Another Eli first. And he kept going! "I feel like I owe you a lot. You're a decent guy, and I'm glad to know you. You, too, Joel."

At which point I fell over. Just to make a point. Eli laughed, "get up, you jerk." Then he reached down to help pull me back up, smirking and shaking his head.

"So, you're feeling okay?" I asked him.

"Actually, I feel great. I don't know, it's like I used to be all wound up about stuff, but now it doesn't feel like any of it was all that important."

"And your head?" I asked.

"Still up there with no leaks," he said.

"Cool!" I said.

There was kind of a pause, and then Eli said, "Jesus, I kind of need to talk to you about something."

"Do you want me to leave?" I asked.

"No," they both said. Something was up.

"It's about Dara," Eli said. "She wasn't sure how to think about the other night, so she came by to talk to me and see how I was doing. And we had a really good talk. And then yesterday we ran into each other at the market, so we hung out for a while."

I could tell Jesus was trying to be cool and not react, but I knew him better than to think this wasn't a tough thing to take.

"So… ," Jesus said.

"So, she asked me to come over and talk to you about… us. Cause last time things didn't go so well between you and Tobiah. And I think she's kind of embarrassed about going from guy to guy."

"Right," Jesus said. "Got it." He started planing down a board so hard, I thought it might catch on fire.

Eli said, "dude, I'm really sorry."

Eli apologizing: thought about falling over again. "I know this sucks," Eli went on. "We both still like you and all. It just kind of happened."

Jesus stopped his work. I'd never seen him look so angry. He didn't say anything, but went over to Eli and looked at him. Just when I thought he was going to throw a punch, he put out his hand. Eli shook his hand, then turned and slowly walked away.

I was wishing I had Jesus' ability to vanish, and wondered if I was in good enough with God to ask, when Jesus said, "what will a man give in exchange for his soul?"

"Huh?" I said. "You sure took that pretty well."

"I try to treat people the way they'd want me to treat them."

"Nice job!"

"The son of man must suffer many things."

"Oh, so now you're gonna feel sorry for yourself?"

"Yes, I believe I will."

"Jesus, c'mon."

"You *really* think you know what it's like to be me?" There was a lot of intensity behind that one.

"Well, excuse *me* for not being on par with a messiah! I don't see any *other* messiahs hanging around."
I wasn't going to take his crap, but it did make me a little nervous to make him mad. "So, I should go?" I asked.
"No, stay. Just don't talk."
"No problem."
"And hand me that hammer."
"Are you going to hit me with it?"
"Maybe later," he said.
"Can't you just ask God to make her like you better?"
"You're still talking."
"Right."

A few days went by, and I saw Dara and Eli walking together in the market, and they looked really happy.
"Hey," I called to them.
"Hi, Joel," Dara said.
"Whassup?" Eli said.
"Shopping?" I asked.
"No, just looking," Eli said. "I already found something I like," and he put his arm around Dara and pulled her in.
She said, "so, I'm a thing, huh?"
"Oh, man, she just never stops!"he said, and they both laughed.
Ezra walked up. They had all planned to meet together. I don't know whose idea it was, but I thought it was pretty cool that they included him.
Eli said to me, "We're going to hack around here for a while – you wanna join us?"

"Nah," I said, "I'm meeting… I'm doing something else." It was still awkward to mention Jesus. I was supposed to meet him at the foot of the path into the hills, so I said goodbye and took off.

When I found Jesus, he had this embarrassed smile on his face.

"Hey, buddy." he said.

"Where's the hammer?" I asked suspiciously.

"Not here," he laughed.

"I just saw Eli, Dara and Ezra in the market together," I said, testing him.

"Huh! That's cool." I guess he really had recovered.

"Hey," he said, "are you still sleeping over at Saul's?"

"No, just the one night."

"I was thinking we should both go over some night. Ya know?"

"Yeah," I said, "I think Saul would like that. But you get the floor."

"Joel, do you really think the floor is the right place for the Messiah to sleep?"

"Okay, here we go; messiah this, messiah that. Ooo, look at me, I'm so special!"

He chased me half-way up the hill before we both collapsed from exhaustion.

"You're really okay about Dara?" I asked, once I'd caught my breath.

"Plenty of fish in the sea, Joel."

"But you still like the one that got away."

He dropped his head. "A wise man once told me, 'where your treasure is, there will your heart be also'."

"And where is your heart?" I asked.

"We'll see. We'll see," he said.

3:7

Zelda arrived yesterday. My dead mom's cousin? Her brother and his wife brought her here, so now there're four adults and me. And they're acting like it's totally normal, even though I can tell they're all nervous as hell. Zelda is being overly nice and a little flirty. Ira and Orpah keep chatting away like monkeys. They must be anxious to get rid of her. She's been living with them since her husband died.

This morning Ira pulled me aside and said that this is a good thing, my dad and Zelda, and that I should be happy and supportive. Gee, thanks for that. What am I, chopped liver that I couldn't figure that out on my own? And who the hell are you (other than my dead mother's cousin who I've never met before) to tell me how I'm supposed to act in my own damn house? Then I remind myself that this is good for Dad - if not so much for me.

But then it hits me. *I could leave!* With my dad all set, I could take off for Caesarea and the sea and Nissa!

That *really* freaked me out. Without an excuse, I'll really have to do it. Leave my home, my town, my friends. Well, the home and town part weren't so tough, but my friends? Sure, we weren't spending so much time together now that Tobiah had taken off, and Eli and Oren had girlfriends. But leave Saul and Jesus? They had become my best friends, and I would feel weird leaving them. Maybe Jesus would want to come with me? Maybe Saul? Hmmm.

That night was the night we'd arranged to sleep over at Saul's house, like Jesus had suggested. I was glad, because it felt so weird at home. Saul's folks had made up a third bed, so I didn't have to try to kick Jesus' ass to get the bed instead of the floor. Is that bad to say about a messiah? Oh well. He would have won anyway.

When we finally went to bed, Saul said, "you guys are awesome to come over."
"How're you doing with Tobiah being gone and everything?" I asked.
"Okay. It still sucks. And in a way, I don't really want to get used to it."
Jesus said, "You'd rather miss him?"
"Yeah," Saul said.
This was the moment.
"Let's say you could have gone with him," I said, "would you have gone?"
Saul had to think about that one. "I don't know! Then I'd miss you guys and everything."

Jesus zeroed in on me and said, "Something on your mind there, Joel?"

"I've been thinking about the sea. And I think I want to go back. Soon. Would you guys want to go with me?"

There was a long pause. I continued, "think about it. We could probably get jobs with Samuel and become fishermen. We'd be out on the sea every day. And he's got all those daughters. It just sounds like such a sweet life to me. The three of us, leaving this dusty little town and living by *the sea!* Tell me that doesn't sound good."

That was my salespitch. More silence as I sweated out the response. I was glad it was dark, cause I really didn't want to see their expressions. It was like the last moment of possibilities before I heard their answers.

Saul finally said, "I like the idea… but I don't know. I think my folks would be sad."

"Yeah," I said, "but you'd say goodbye and tell them where you're going. It would be totally different from Tobiah."

Jesus asked, "are you for sure going?"

"I feel like now's the time."

"Is this because of Zelda?" Jesus asked.

"It's more than that. It's like you and your mission. It somehow feels inevitable."

"Have you really given her a chance?"

I didn't much like Jesus' response about Zelda. Now I had to look deep inside myself and blah, blah, blah.

Saul said, "I don't think I liked the sea as much as you guys did. But I'll think about it!"
I rolled over and tried to go to sleep. Stupid Jesus.

So the next day, Zelda asks me to go to the market with her, like she just came up with the idea. Sheah, right. They'd probably planned this all night. Then I remembered what Jesus had said, and I agreed to go.

As we're walking around the market, she says, "tell me a little about yourself."
Shoot me now. "Uhh... ," I said, "like, what do you want to know?"
"Is there a special girl in your life?"
"Sort of."
Oh, man. I'd rather pull my own ears off with a pair of tongs. It went on and on like that, and I kept feeling like everything I did was small and boring. Then I had to go home and help her cook, while Ira, Orpah and my dad all whispered in the next room. I mean, she's nice enough, but…

Dinner was okay. She's not even a bad cook. And we actually had a few laughs. Then they dropped the bomb.

"Joel," Ira says, "you should come back with us for a few days. You'll have fun!" Translation;
"you should let Zelda and Dad have some alone time." That kind of did it. That was when I knew for

sure I was going back to Caesarea in the next few months. I didn't really answer their invitation, but I think they got the message.

Next day in the hills:

"Jesus," I asked, "is it okay to ask for things from God? I mean, does He Listen, or am I like a dog howling at the moon?"

"It kind of depends on what you ask for."

"That's weird."

"Think about it. If you ask for your 'boatload of cash,' He won't hear that. What He'll hear is a whiny child."

"Thanks."

"But," he continued, "if you ask for a bigger heart or getting closer to Him… "

"So He's only going to hear me when I ask for things He actually gives."

"Something like that, yeah," Jesus said. "What are you asking for?"

I took me awhile to whittle it down. "Direction, I guess. So I just ask Him?"

"Ask and you will receive an answer. It might not be the answer you want, though."

"Crap!" I said.

"Yeah, tell me about it. Reveal to me what's in your heart, brother"

"Huh?"

"Reveal to me what's in your heart, brother"

"Why are you talking like that?"

"I don't know, I'm trying to sound more Messiah-like."

"It sounds pretty dorky is what it sounds like."

Jesus sighed. "What's up, man?" he asked in his peeved voice.

"Now you're ticked at me."

"Joel?"

"Alright. I want to go to the sea. And I want to get to know Nissa. Honestly, I'd really like to kiss her in the moonlight and maybe even… "

"Whoa there, tiger, I get the picture."

"Sometimes I feel like there's so much I want, and it kills me to have to wait to see if I ever even get it."

"I want the world to live in peace. You know how long *that's* going to take? Three thousand years."

"Damn! Wait, really?"

"Yeah, really. Joel, here's my advice: just move forward. You'll know what's right when you need to."

"That's it? 'Move forward'?"

"Yep."

It was both comforting in its simplicity, and not. I suddenly felt kind of scared. Well, not really scared, but alone.

"Come with me to Caesarea." I blurted out.

Jesus looked at the ground. "I'd like to. I really would. But not yet."

It was weird. It suddenly felt like we were walking along the seashore on a bright sunny morning. I said out loud, "this is where I belong," and just as sudden, we were back in the hills above Nazareth. "Yes," Jesus said, "I think so, too."

I shook my head. If that wasn't God…

"Were you just showing off?" I asked Jesus. "Cause you said you weren't allowed to do that."

"Nope. That was just me being me." And he smiled.

Right about then, Mordecai comes walking up the path. I don't know what Jesus felt, but I tensed up, ready for a fight.

"There you guys are," Mordecai said. "I heard you come up here all the time."

"What do you want?" I asked.

"I kinda wanted to talk to Jesus," he said. "If that's okay."

"Sure, go ahead," Jesus said.

Mordecai looked at me like I was supposed to leave, but I didn't. "Okay," he said. "There's a rumor going around that you healed Eli and Ezra. Is that true?"

"Where did you hear that?" I asked. Mordecai didn't answer.

Jesus asked him, "does it make a difference how it happened?"

"No," he answered, "I guess not."

"So what's your real question?" Jesus asked.

Mordecai looked around with this pained expression on his face, like he was looking for a place to hurl or something. He started to walk
away, then came back and quietly said' "I don't understand."

"I'm sorry, what did you say?" Jesus asked.

"I don't understand!" he yelled.

"What don't you understand?"

"This! You! That stupid kid! What I'm supposed to do!" He was pissed.

"Well, not try to kill people, for starters," I put in.

"But then why does it say they *should* be put to death?"

"Have you talked to the rabbis?" Jesus asked.

"They don't know shit! All they care about is how clean I get the floor of the fucking temple."

"So you felt like you were doing the right thing?" Jesus asked. "There was nothing in it for you?"

"I DON'T KNOW! It doesn't make any fucking sense!" Mordecai glared at us. "Guess you're just not interested in helping normal guys like me." Then he spat on the ground and walked back down the path.

After he was out of earshot, I said, "that was weird."

Jesus said, "he's trying. Gotta give him credit for that."

"I don't know. I'm kinda surprised you even talked to him. He tried to kill our friends."

Jesus gave me a funny look. "You never wanted to kill someone?"

"What are you saying?"

"None of us are perfect."

"Except you?" I asked.

He busted up laughing. "Are you *kidding* me?"

3:8

It was kinda weird. All of us (except Tobiah, of course) were together for the first time in a long while. And we didn't even plan it! We all sort of bumped into each other and started walking towards the river.

Saul had decided it was time for *him* to have a girlfriend, too. But he wasn't sure who. All the girls kind of like him, since he's nice looking and funny and not real bright, so he pretty much has his choice.

Saul: Maybe I could have like a contest or something.
Me: Based on…?
Saul: How big…nah, that would never work. Umm. Best kisser? Best cook! Nicest smile?
Ezra: Attraction is more than how someone looks.
Me: Yeah, isn't there one girl who you really like being with and talking to?
Saul: Hannah. And Judith. Oh, and Freyda. Tamar?
Eli: Dude, it's not like a quiz. It's all about chemistry.
Oren: It's also about fate, I think. When it's the right one you're kind of destined to be together.
Eli: Slow down, Oren, he's not getting married yet, like you. He just wants a girlfriend.
Oren: You never know!
Ezra: Okay, try this. Which one would you want to spend a whole day with?
Saul thought about it. "Freyda."
Me: There you go.
Saul: Or Judith. But Tamar would be cool, too.
Eli: Saul, I don' think you get it. It's like when I first really talked to Dara, we just had this spark.
Oren: Yeah, like there's kind of a natural pull towards her.
We all looked at Eli, expecting him to say something gross. "What?" he said. "I didn't say anything."
Saul: Maybe I could date all of them at once, and just sort of see what happens?

Eli: They'd gang up on you and kick your ass is what would happen.

Saul: Man! Why does this have to be so hard?

We snickered and looked at Eli again. "*What*?" he said. "Oh. Yeah, I get it: funny." But he didn't say it.

Saul: Jesus, could you do something?

Jesus: Like what?

Saul: You know, with your special powers and stuff?

Jesus: If I had a power like that, do you think I'd be sitting here with you guys?

When Jesus gets all snooty like that, it's almost funny.

Saul: What is *wrong* with me?

Ezra: There is nothing wrong with you. You just haven't found the right person yet. Girl. The right girl yet.

Eli went over to Ezra and gave him a friendly noogie.

Saul: Maybe I need to kind of announce that I'm in the market.

Me: Like how?

Oren: Announce it in the market?

Ezra: How about this: how about we combine the contest idea *and* the market idea.

Saul: Yeah?

Ezra: We gather all the girls in the market, and let them chase you, and whoever catches you wins.

Saul: Yeah! I kinda like that!

Ezra: Only you'd be naked. Oh. Did I say that out loud?

Saul started laughing. "That would be crazy! I like it!"

Oren: Saul, you can't stand in the market naked.

Eli got this sly smile on his face. "Unless he was forced to by unnamed pranksters."

Saul: What? Wait, *I'm* naked?

Saul started laughing nervously. "Guys, c'mon, that's crazy!"

Oren: I thought you liked crazy.

Eli, Oren and I grabbed Saul and started hauling him towards town. He was scared, but laughing the whole way. We hadn't planned this or anything, so we just took him behind a building, pulled his robe off and shoved him into the market area. He ran through the market in his underwear, whooping at the top of his lungs, and when he happened to run by Shayna, he grabbed her and kissed her, whooped again, and ran all the way home.

Back by the river, Ezra had a conversation with Jesus. Ezra filled me in later.

Ezra said, "Jesus, am I an abomination if I like guys more than girls?"

Jesus said, "no. Not at all. You already know that."

"It doesn't make me very popular, though."

"What is it you really want, Ezra?"

"Love."

"And where does that come from?"

"God?"

"Ultimately, yeah, I think so. When do you feel love?"

"When I'm with my parents; most of the time, anyway. When I cook. When I see you guys."

"Would that love be there without you there?"

"No, I guess not."

"That's how important you are. Love needs you, too."

"Huh. What about when you *don't* feel love?

"Then I rely on faith."

"Easy for you to say."

"It doesn't take much," Jesus said. "What's the smallest thing you can think of?"

"A raisin."

"Less."

"Sesame seed?"

"Smaller."

"There's not much that's smaller than that. Well, there's a mustard seed. Those things are tiny."

"Yep. That's about right," Jesus said.

"That's it?"

"That's all it takes."

"Are you really the Messiah?"

"We'll see."

"What do *you* really want?"

Jesus sighed. "A little more time."

"But more than a mustard seed."

"A lot more," he said.

Turns out Oren, Eli and Ezra were *all* right. It's chemistry, impulse *and* fate. Shayna found Saul later that day and came right up and kissed him back. She told him that she always kind of liked him, and she thought his underwear run through the market was the kind of spontaneity that she was looking for in a guy. You may remember that Tobiah was sort of interested in Shayna awhile back, because she's really pretty and not real bright. It was almost like Saul and Shayna were perfect for each other, but no one had ever thought of them together before.

Saul's dad heard about the market run from several unhappy townfolks, so he told them that Saul was still a little crazy from his brother having taken off. But to Saul he said, "I'm glad you're feeling better, son, and it's good to let off a little steam sometimes. But next time, keep your clothes on, okay?"

I saw Saul and Shayna a few days later. They were having a serious conversation.

"Saul, where do birds go when it rains?"

"Gosh, babe, I don't know. They have nests and stuff, right?"

"Yeah, but nests don't have roofs. They're like little boats."

"Yeah, I never thought about that. Maybe they flip them over and use them for cover?"

"Saul," Shayna laughed, "how can they pick them up? They have wings, not hands! You are so funny!"

"Yeah? Thanks. You like funny, right?"

She kissed him. And they kept on kissing, so I took off.

On the home front, Zelda, Ira and Orpah had finally left, and it was just me and my dad.

"So how did you like Zelda?" my dad asked.

"She's nice."

"And?"

"And?"

"*And…?*"

"And… she's a pretty good cook," I said.

"*Pretty* good? Apparently my cooking has destroyed any sense of taste you might have had. For that I apologize. I'm thinking of asking her to marry me."
I didn't say anything.
"Joel!" he shouted.
"What?"
"Enough with the teenage sullenness! Tell me what you're thinking!"
"Alright!"
"I'm your father, I shouldn't have to ask like this! And you're not stupid, you know what this means."
I was getting really hot inside. I didn't like him calling me out like this.

"It doesn't matter to me," was all I could get out.
"It doesn't matter? Well it *should* matter! It's your home!"
That did it. "No, Dad, it's *your* home, and now it's yours and *Zelda's* home, and I don't really know why you're bothering to ask me, because you're going to go through with it either way!" I'd never yelled at my dad before.
"That's not true, it's why I'm asking you now!" He'd never really yelled at me before, either.
"No, because if I say I don't like her, you'll just say, 'give it a chance, I'm sure you'll like her once you get to know her better'." I used my lower "dad voice" just to drive home the point.
"Well, it's true! You *will* get to like her!"
"No, I won't! And it doesn't matter because I'm leaving anyway!" Oops.
"What's this? Where do you think *you're* going?"

"Back to Caesarea. As soon as possible." There was a pause.

His voice was really quiet now. "And when were you going to inform me of this decision?"

"I don't know. I've been meaning to," I said.

"Tobiah was no surprise, but you, I thought you had more sense."

"I *belong* there."

"Says who? You didn't ask me."

"*I* say so. And so does Jesus." I'm not sure why I threw that in. I guess I was hoping at least one other opinion would help my cause.

"Pffff!" my dad said. "That crazy kid? I wouldn't base any decision on what *he* says."

I could feel myself getting hot again. I was mad that he dissed my friend, and stunned that maybe there was this opinion among the parents that Jesus was crazy. Had I said something? I didn't think so. And I was pretty surprised that I no longer thought of Jesus as crazy. I really believed he was something special.

"Fine," he said. "I was hoping to give you more of a family, something I haven't been able to do by myself, but apparently, it's too late."

"Dad. I don't *need* a family. I've been perfectly happy with you."

"No. The reason you haven't needed a family is because you already have one."

"What do you mean?"

"Those boys, the ones you're always hanging around with. I'm not sure about some of them, but I didn't say anything, hoping I'd raised you well enough that you could figure things out for yourself. That's your so-called family."

Man. Here I thought I was telling him what was what, and now I felt like crap.
After a long time, he said, "I'll miss you."
I left the house and didn't get back till I was sure he'd already gone to bed.

3:9

So now it was just us bachelors; Ezra, Jesus and I. We talked Ezra into going up into the hills with us, and he said he'd make us dinner afterward.

Ezra: So when are you leaving?
Me: Day after tomorrow.
Jesus: And you'll go try to find Samuel at the beach?
Me: Yeah. It's weird. I've been looking forward to this the whole time I couldn't go, and now that I'm going, I'm not so sure.
Jesus: Remember what I said; move forward. Even if it means staying here.
Me: See, I can't stay here. My dad practically said I should leave.
Ezra: Really?
Me: The last thing he said to me was 'I'll miss you.'
Ezra: Maybe he was just trying to shock you.
Me: He didn't say it like that. He said it like it was a done deal.
Jesus: When did he say that?

Me: Two days ago.
Ezra: And you haven't talked since?
Me: Nope. He hasn't said anything either.
Ezra: You're going to say goodbye to him, right?
Me: Yeah, I guess.

Ezra gave me a look.

Me: Yes, I'll say goodbye.
Ezra: Good. You won't regret it.
Me: (to Jesus) Did you ever talk to Dara?
Jesus: Yeah, we're cool. I think she was too smart for me anyway.
Me: It's not like you're stupid. Crazy maybe, but not stupid.
Jesus: Oh, thanks. I didn't say I was stupid.

I thought about what my dad had said about him.

Me: You're not stupid. And you're not crazy either. I believe you are a prophet.
Ezra: Me, too.
Jesus looked at us. He smiled, but he seemed kind of sad somehow.

Dinner that night was great. Nothing as huge as our other meals, but good anyway. It was cool to hang out with just Ezra and Jesus. At the end of it, Ezra gave me a little packet.
"It's empty," I said.
"No," he said, "there's one mustard seed in it. For luck."
They are *really* small.

The next day, my dad finally broke the silence.

"You leave tomorrow?" he asked.

"Yeah."

"Me, too. I'm going to see Zelda. I hope she'll have me."

"Should be an easier sell with me gone."

"Son, I understand you feel like you have to do this, but don't blame me for it."

"I'm not! I've been thinking about this ever since I *left* Caesarea. I just didn't want to hurt you."

He thought about that a long time.

"I have some things I'd like to give you."

He went into the closet and brought out an old wooden box. He opened it and handed me a scarf. "This was your mother's. Obviously you can't wear it, but I thought you might like to have it anyway. And here's some money. It's not much, but it will get you through a week or two, if you're careful with it."

"Thanks."

"Will you come back and visit?"

"No. You have to come visit me," I said with a smirk. "The sea is incredible."

He smiled and put out his arms. So we hugged and were cool again.

When I got to my room, I smelled the scarf, hoping to find a memory of her. It was just barely there, hidden under and mixed with the old wood smell of the box. It made me all nostalgic.

So I started walking around town, remembering all the times I'd had. The well, where we all usually met up, and where Jesus had filled up the waterbag so we could get the donkeys drunk. The river, where Hannah and her hot cousin Martha from Irbid had tricked us into taking off our clothes, and Tobiah had yelled at
Jesus. The field, where we used to lie out under the stars, and where Jesus first disappeared.
The tree, where I overheard Jesus and Ezra, and then Jesus and Dara. The temple, where we first found Ezra, and Eli got caught by the rabbi. The market, where the soldier had grabbed the egg, and Saul did his almost naked run.

Jesus found me there at the market, so we went up into the hills one last time. When we got to the top, he said, "How are you doing?"
"Man. I'm like eighteen different things at once," I said.
"You'll be fine. You're smart, you're a good guy, and an even better friend."
Wow! "Thanks."
"I wish I could tell you how much your friendship has meant to me, but I'm afraid you'll get all mushy and start crying."
"Shut up," I said. "Same here. Are *you* going to be okay? I mean with God and everything?"
"Yeah, I think so."
"Hopefully you'll get in a couple more girlfriends before you have to start that whole messiah business."
"From your mouth to God's ear! When do you leave?"

"First thing in the morning."

"Can I send you off?"

"Sure. Meet me at the well."

"You're not going to pull a Tobiah and diss me are you?"

"No," I laughed, "I'll be there."

I actually slept that night. I was kinda surprised when I woke up and the sky was already beginning to lighten. But I took that as a good sign.

When I got to the well, it wasn't just Jesus; *all* the guys were there, as well as Dara, Leah and Shayna. I got all choked up just seeing them standing there. Eli was even there on time.

"Hey, there he is!" Eli said.

I looked at Jesus, who said, "turns out some other people wanted to say goodbye, too."

I tried to say something, but nothing came out.

Oren spoke up. "Here's to Joel, our brave and excellent friend. May he have sunny skies and smooth sailing."

Everyone said, "to Joel!"

Ezra said, "*Now* can we have a group hug?"

We all kinda smooshed together.

Saul said, "all right, dude. Go chase that dream!"

So I did.

3:10

Hey. It's been a long, long time, but here I am again. I have just one more story about a particularly good day I had.

We had pulled in a good haul. Great weather, too. That rarely happens, so when it does, the whole family feels good. We were stretching out the nets to look for rips, when off in the distance, I saw some guy walking along the
shore. So I just got up and started walking towards him. When I got close enough, he looked at me and said, "Joel."
"Holy shit – Jesus!" I said.
He laughed, "you haven't changed a bit."
We gave each other a big hug.
"How long has it been?" I asked.
"Don't even think about it. You're looking well."
"You, too. Nice beard."
"You, too."
"I've been hearing about you. Well, I've been hearing about this Jesus the Christ, and I kinda figured. Things going well?"
"Ups and downs, but yeah, I'm getting the job done."
"Nice, good for you."
"And you're happy?" he asked.
"Very. It's a lot tougher life than I'd thought, but Nissa and the kids – oh yeah, I married Nissa."
"Kids? You?"
"Yeah, crazy huh? Four of them! But it's good."

We just stood and looked at each other.

"Remember when we were first here together?" I asked.

"Very much so," he said. "That was quite a day."

"Can you stay for dinner?"

"No, I have to meet up with my disciples. They get a little lost when they're left alone for very long."

"Kind of like all of us in the old days, huh?"

"No, this is quite a bit different. But it's a good group. You wouldn't want to join us, would you?"

"You mean for dinner?"

Jesus laughed, "no. Come be one of my disciples."

I was stunned. "I'm not really, I mean, my family... and I don't know that I'm all that good at religion."

"But you believe," he said." And you have a good heart."

I smiled. "Sorry, man. This is my life now."

He smiled back. "Fair enough. But you're always welcome."

We stood and looked at each other again.

He said, "I kinda have to... "

"Yeah," I said, "me, too."

Watching him walk away, I felt really proud of him.

The End

Made in the USA
Columbia, SC
24 March 2021